BISON
BOOKS

D0838811

JULES VERNE

Lighthouse at the End of the World

Le Phare du bout du monde

The First English Translation of Verne's Original Manuscript

Translated and edited by William Butcher

UNIVERSITY OF NEBRASKA PRESS • LINCOLN

Publication of this book was made possible by a grant from
The Florence Gould Foundation.

Le Phare du bout du monde © Les Éditions internationales
Alain Stanké, 1999. © Editions de l'Archipel. Translation
and critical apparatus © 2007 by William Butcher.

Library of Congress Cataloging-in-Publication Data
Verne, Jules, 1828–1905.
[Le phare du bout du monde. English]
Lighthouse at the end of the world = Le phare du bout
du monde : the first English translation of Verne's original
manuscript / Jules Verne ; translated and edited by
William Butcher.
p. cm. — (Bison frontiers of imagination)
Includes bibliographical references.
ISBN-13: 978-0-8032-4676-8 (cloth : alk. paper)
ISBN-13: 978-0-8032-6007-8 (pbk. : alk. paper)
I. Butcher, William, 1951– II. Title. III. Title: Le phare
du bout du monde.
PQ2469.P4E5 2007
843'.8—dc22
2007001717

Set in Adobe Garamond by Kim Essman.
Designed by R. W. Boeche.

CONTENTS

INTRODUCTION

Lighthouse at the End of the World (1905) by Jules Verne (1828–1905) is not well known in the English-speaking world, yet this gripping adventure story set on the remotest of islands deserves much better. Before studying its composition, characters, and themes, it is useful to summarize the plot and examine Verne's life at the turn of the century.

ABBREVIATIONS

BSJV	*Bulletin de la Société Jules Verne*
Gallica	Text available on the Gallica website of the Bibliothèque nationale de France, gallica.bnf.fr
JV	Jules Verne, used to indicate his own notes or in contradistinction to MV
MÉR	*Magasin d'éducation et de recréation*
MS	Jules Verne's manuscript, the basis for the present edition
MV	Edition of *Lighthouse* published in 1905, written by Jules Verne and revised by Michel Verne
OED	Oxford English Dictionary

PLOT

In 1859 the Argentine sloop *Santa Fe* leaves Vasquez, Felipe, and Moriz on deserted, near-polar Staten Island. They are to tend the new lighthouse at Elgor Bay, and hence protect the world's ships. But a gang of wreckers, led by the diabolical Kongre and Carcante, have long been stranded here. The merciless pirates hoist a light to lure the schooner *Maule* onto the reefs, killing all hands. In order to repair the vessel and thus escape to the South Seas, the wreckers sail her to Elgor Bay. While a powerless Vasquez observes from the lighthouse, they kill the trusting Felipe and Moriz. Unable to leave the island, the keeper needs to avoid his enemies while waiting for the sloop to return. The pirates draw in an American ship, killing all on board except First Officer John Davis. After bad weather slows the repairs, Vasquez and Davis, who have jointly sworn revenge, further delay the *Maule* using a salvaged cannon. The pirates are finally leaving the bay at dusk—when the *Santa Fe* hoves into sight. The climax involves much drama and bloodshed.

BIOGRAPHY

Verne's fascination for Latin America was visible from his childhood. His family holidayed in the idyllic French countryside at the house of his great-uncle Prudent Allotte de la Fuÿe. Uncle Prudent, a retired slaver, had done business in Venezuelan trading ports— and the boy idolized him for traveling so far. Verne's earliest prose publication was "The First Ships of the Mexican Navy," and his third, "Martin Paz," was set in Peru.

Verne's life and career are useful for understanding *Lighthouse*. However, the main events are outlined in the Chronology (pp. xxxiii–xxxviii), so we should proceed directly to the final years.

Since 1886, when his publisher and mentor had died and a premeditated murder attempt by his favorite nephew had left him permanently lame, Verne's life had entered a spiral of decline, with increasing isolation and plummeting popularity.

The novelist turned staunchly conservative, being anti-Dreyfusard in the 1896 Affair; the same year he was sued for libel. His contemporaries died one by one: his younger brother Paul in 1897, his traveling companion Aristide Hignard in 1898, his family maid in 1900, his great love and first cousin Caroline Dezaunay in 1901.

Verne's last journey was in 1899, to Les Petites-Dalles on the Normandy coast, with his son Michel and Michel's family (Dusseau, 483). He resigned from the Paris Society of Geography and skipped the Universal Exposition (1900)—including the first Metro. That same year, he and his wife moved out of rented accommodation at 2 Rue Charles Dubois, Amiens, and back to their own dark and cramped 44 Boulevard de Longueville. The furniture huddled in the dining and living rooms and the "tiny garden [was] invaded by sparrows" (Jules-Verne, x). On the first floor, Verne's study had just "two tables, a padded armchair, and a camp bed" (Jules-Verne, x).

The novelist's health deteriorated. On 15 October 1898, he wrote to his sister, "I'm living off milk and eggs and my legs are useless with rheumatism." With increasing hunger pangs from the diabetes that would kill him, he could not wait for meals, but ate alone, sitting on a stool so as "to go faster" (Jules-Verne, x). To the cataract in his left eye was added one in his right. Canceling the needed operation in 1900 made him "very distressed": "I can scarcely see what I'm writing."[1] In March 1901 a nasty flu kept him in his room for two months; he was "very, very ill" (*Entretiens*, 146). His presence, taking refuge in silence, "more aged than really old," terrified his future biographer Jean Jules-Verne, aged nine—except when he animatedly discussed his books with Jean's father Michel (Jules-Verne, x). From 1902 his condition worsened, his "words run[ning] away and ideas no longer com[ing]," and many journalists departed disappointed. In 1903 "the only time he went out was for his short constitutional."[2]

Yet Verne struggled on through the growing gloom. He had been triumphantly reelected in the Amiens municipal elections of 1900, although now nodding off in meetings and speaking less and less. In 1902 he was still rising at four o'clock to write for seven hours.[3] Not only did he compose the first draft of *Lighthouse* between March and May 1901, but on occasion he could still appear "upright, like the master he is . . . [within] his eyes . . . a singular vivacity" (*Entretiens*, 146).

And still the books kept pouring out: *The Mighty Orinoco* (1898), about a search for a river source; *The Will of an Eccentric* (1899), a board game across the United States, still unpublished there today; the anti-Robinsonade *Second Homeland* (1900); the missing-link *Village in the Treetops* (1901); the sea-monster *Yarns of Jean-Marie Cabidoulin* (1901); the judicial error embroiling the *Kip Brothers* (1902); *Traveling Scholarships* (1903), about touring the West Indies; *A Drama in Livonia* (1904), featuring German-Slav rivalry; *Master of the World* (1904), where a megalomaniac Robur-the-Conqueror returns in a car-plane-sub; *Invasion of the Sea* (1905), about flooding the Sahara.

Yet others were composed, creating a backlog, for only one or two could come out each year: *Magellania*, where the solitude-seeking hero has to rule castaways; "The Secret of Wilhelm Storitz," about an invisible man; "The Beautiful Yellow Danube," sailing across central Europe; *The Meteor Hunt*, featuring a gold-bearing asteroid; "The Golden Volcano," set in the Klondyke; and four and a half chapters of "Study Visit," set in French colonial Africa.

On 17 March 1905, the only universal Frenchman fell ill, dying on 24 March, surrounded by his extended family. The French government did not attend the funeral.

SOURCES

The idea for the eponymous lighthouse probably came from the first one in the South Atlantic, the real-life beacon built in Port San Juan (1884). While both were inexplicably positioned behind eight-hundred-foot ranges, and so invisible from most ships, the differences are more important than the similarities.[4] Whereas Verne's beacon is the classic stone-built cylinder, with a range of eight to ten miles, the one-story wooden lighthouse of 1884 was polygonal, with a banal galvanized roof but a range of fourteen miles. While the novel talks loftily of benefiting sailors of every nation, in reality the motive was territorial, to shore up Argentina's brand-new, still disputed, sovereignty.[5]

Otherwise, the genesis of *Lighthouse* is largely terra incognita. Bougainville's *Voyage around the World* (1772) could be a slight source, given that rare terms like "guanacos" and "Pécherais" occur. The novelist may have known of Darwin's visit to "the rugged and inhospitable cliffs of Statenland." He perhaps read about a herculean Finn called Iwan Iwanowsky, deserter from the Argentine Navy, who escaped from prison in Port San Juan three times between 1881 and 1885, provoking admiration at his survival, although finally succumbing to cold and starvation.[6] Verne was presumably aware of the visit to Staten Island in 1899 of Adrien Gerlache and Roald Amundsen's Antarctic expedition.[7] Some of Verne's information on Patagonia was supplied by an unidentified lady correspondent in "deepest Argentina."[8]

No other plausible sources have been suggested. Verne's Extraordinary Voyages were published as a series, with many recurring themes and situations. It may consequently be more fruitful to explore these recurrent variations, one convenient way being to simultaneously study the genre, or rather genres, the novel belongs to.

Lighthouse is, firstly, a Robinsonade; the castaway genre best describes Verne, infinitely more than the inaccurate science fiction label stuck on him from the 1920s—long after he was able to defend himself. Desert islands obsessed him from childhood, for the ten-year-old sailed a skiff down the Loire, sank on an island, and played at being a solitary castaway until hunger drove him home again.[9] His only known early reading was Robinsonades: Mallès de Beaulieu's "Twelve-Year-Old Crusoe," Louis Desnoyers' "Adventures of Robert Robert," and Ernest Fouinet's "Crusoe of the Ice," followed by Johann Rudolf Wyss's *Swiss Family Robinson*, Defoe's *Robinson Crusoe*, and Fenimore Cooper's *The Crater*. Verne later read Captain Marryat, Mayne Reid, and Robert Louis Stevenson, especially *Treasure Island*, with its "extraordinary freshness of style and enormous power," but also *The Ebb-Tide* and, significantly, *The Wrecker* (*Entretiens*, 105).

Lighthouse is, secondly, a marine novel. Large numbers of Verne's books demonstrate his passion for navigation, which emerges even in the Center of the Earth, At the North Pole, or Off on a Comet. This novel remains true to type, with undoubtedly the widest range of nautical terms and themes of any of the works, paradoxically enough as it never leaves Staten. It thus parallels Verne's own life, stranded on dry land after he gave up sailing in 1884.

The novel is, lastly, defined by the island's role as gateway to the Antarctic. Verne had long been fascinated by the Poles, the last virgin expanses on the globe. In 1851 he visited an uncle in Dunkirk, a major port for Arctic whalers, and subsequently wrote "Wintering in the Ice" (1855). The northern urge also dominates Verne's 1859 journey, his first identified outside France. In the Scottish chapters of his *Backwards to Britain*, the hero, the Count of the North, constantly dreams of penetrating ever further into the Highlands. In 1861 Verne traveled for five weeks, missing the birth of his only child, Michel. The resultant account, "Joyous Miseries of Three Travelers in Scandinavia," contains a lifelong manifesto: "I was drawn to the hyperboreal regions, like the magnetic needle to the north, without knowing why . . . I love cold lands by temperament." Verne equates altitude with latitude and the delicious chill, three scales measuring out his search for the absolute. He especially indulges his mesmeric obsession in three novels set entirely in the icy wastes: *The Adventures of Captain Hatteras* (1864), *The Fur Country* (1873), and *An Antarctic Mystery* (1897).

Both Poles shared the conundrum of whether they were land or sea, the first new continent since 1606 or the open polar ocean proposed by Sir Francis Drake (*Grant*, I ix). While hundreds of expeditions had assaulted the Arctic, the South Pole came into vogue more slowly. In 1901 the melded dreams of a classical temperate Hyperborea and a Terra Australis Incognita burned as strongly as ever amongst scholars and cranks. Blended in were wild substrata of utopias, whether founded by Europeans to escape society's ills or preexisting, unsullied communities.

This was where Staten Island came in. *Lighthouse* may in fact have been a spin-off from *Magellania*, written in 1898 but published only in 1909 (radically altered by Michel Verne). The two novels cover the same geographical area, the same flora and fauna, the same ports; both emphasize the danger of shipwreck and the misery of the "Fuegians" or "Pécherais"; and both revel in the inhospitality of the terrain and the fact that it remains independent of all sovereignty. *Magellania* closes with the erection of a lighthouse on an island, explicitly compared to "the light on Staten Island" (xvi). *Lighthouse* opens with an identical image—and indeed closes again with it. The triple depiction of the structure defying the world may symbolize the fight against the darkness invading Verne's eyesight and mind—against the grim reaper.

As the writer points out in *The First Explorers* (1870), Tasman discovered a "Staten Land" in 1642, part, he thought, of a great southern continent (it was later rebaptized New Zealand). Tasman and Darwin's use of the same geographical term for land at opposite ends of the earth shows the extent of the imagined continent and the grip it held on the global imagination.

Staten Island, the remotest tip of the known continents, formed the obligatory staging post for the many cumbersome *fin-de-siècle* expeditions into the southern unknown. Together with neighboring South Georgia, the island resembled Siberia or Greenland in both climate and tantalizing otherness, a lingering whiteness on the map, an idealistic hope it might stay independent for ever, blended with the selfish dream of printing one's name on the virginal expanse.

Verne's problem, though, is that he has already been to both Poles, in *Hatteras* and *Twenty Thousand Leagues*. In a fallen century where there are no discoveries left, Staten thus represents the derisory least bad solution, a mocking memory of geographical heroism, a spin-off from an already lost dream. Despite the no-man's land's extreme latitude and weather, despite its brave last stand against the colonial empires, it is in many ways a retreat. Travel is pointless for everything has been done. All Verne's islands represent this pitiful inversion of the voyage—the aim of his life and works. Staten can be seen as both the culmination and the denial of the polar urge, both a new discovery and the reluctant recognition that salvation can no longer be sought through geography. *Lighthouse* is a dream of elsewhere tempered for a bourgeois century.

COMPOSITION

While the inspiration for *Lighthouse* remains a black box, we do have information about its path to publication. On 29 March 1901, three years after *Magellania*, Verne finished writing "The Beautiful Yellow Danube." That same day, he began *Lighthouse*, completing the draft on 17 May.[10]

Jean Jules-Verne (*Jules Verne*, 346) claims the novel was written during a period of depression, but may simply be arguing from its somber tone. Examination of the manuscript shows that, as usual, Verne inked over his pencil draft, then made a few minor deletions and insertions; with an increasing backlog of unpublished novels, he normally did the ink version several years after the pencil one.[11] His errors betrayed his failing eyesight and fatigue, with words incorrectly crossed out; the writing, however, remains nearly as well formed as ever.[12] As in the previous manuscripts, there are a few gaps for distances, technical words, etc.[13]

On 25 February 1905 we have the first mention of *Lighthouse* in Verne's extant correspondence. He told Hetzel fils, his publisher since 1886: "I will soon send you the manuscript. It will probably not be the one I mentioned, 'The Invisible Man' ('L'Invisible'), but *Lighthouse at the End of the World*, set on the last tip of Tierra del Fuego."

In addition to *Invasion of the Sea*, which had started coming out in Hetzel's *Magasin d'éducation et de recréation* (MÉR) on 1 January, another book was needed for August. On 4 March Hetzel wrote to confirm receipt of the manuscript, later remarking that although he had not actually read it, the title itself was "destined to succeed."[14] However, he continued, it would "overshadow" the title of *Invasion of the Sea*, so it was perhaps "stupid" to publish them in the same annual volume. He enquired whether Verne could send "The Invisible Man." Verne replied on 5 March that he had posted *Lighthouse* because he thought there would not be changes to it. But he agreed to send what he preferred to call "Storitz's Secret." On 12 March Hetzel confirmed he had received the new manuscript, but said he had to leave for Italy, having left instructions for it to be copied, so he could read it on his return (BSJV, 103:40).

On 24 March Verne died. Clearly he considered the manuscript finished—qua manuscript. But he had earlier pointed out: "I consider my real labor begins with my first set of proofs, for I not only correct something in every sentence, but rewrite whole chapters."[15] However, "with age and infirmity there were some books . . . which Verne did not [revise intensively on proofs] and their sales suffered" (Hetzel fils's note in May 1905, in BSJV, 104:5). In sum, Verne would certainly have made many changes to *Lighthouse* at the successive proof stages.

On 30 April Michel Verne wrote a letter to *Le Figaro* and *Le Temps*, referring to eight manuscript works, including one volume of stories, but mentioning only three actual titles.[16] All eight were in his physical possession, except *Lighthouse* and "Storitz."[17]

Who now owned the right to bring out the eight works, and these two in particular? Hetzel stated that he "had been charged by M. Jules Verne to publish [the eight posthumous works, including *Lighthouse*], while retaining the author's text as much as possible, except where there were mistakes" (*BSJV*, 104:19).[18] On 9 May the publisher wrote to Michel that he could not return the manuscripts of *Lighthouse* and "Storitz," as requested, since Verne had sent them for publication—and that Verne's son could contact a lawyer if he wished (*BSJV*, 103:40). The following day a visibly upset Michel countered that on his deathbed his father had explained why he had submitted two manuscripts, saying that his son could do as he wished with them (*BSJV*, 103:42). Michel also referred to his father's will, which read: "I hereby bequeath all my manuscripts, books, maps, library, and papers, without exception . . . to my son Michel Verne" (Martin, 252). (The location of Verne's will, of vital importance for understanding both his life and works, has surprisingly not been identified.) In sum, the manuscripts belonged to Michel and he had the power to refuse publication. Hetzel responded on 11 May that he was consulting his own lawyer, and attached a "Note concerning the manuscript *Lighthouse at the End of the World*," summarizing the epistolary exchanges of early March (*BSJV*, 103:43–45). He maintained that he had the right to bring *Lighthouse* out (although later agreeing to return "Storitz" [*BSJV*, 103:50]). At this point, although he seems to have been legally and morally in the right, Michel gave in.

On 25 June, perhaps heartened by a handsome publisher's check, he wrote about a backup copy of the manuscript of *Lighthouse*: "I read [it] this morning. I realized that it needed very few changes, all of small details." He added he would start "correcting" it as a matter of urgency.[19] *Lighthouse* was then serialized in the *MÉR*, from 15 August to 15 December. The first publication in volume form was in about November, with the copyright date surprisingly indicated as "29 July 1905"; the text had been slightly revised from the *MÉR*.[20]

Hetzel fils and Verne fils signed a contract in March 1906 covering *Lighthouse* and the seven other manuscripts. It stipulated notably that "Mr. Michel Jules Verne undertakes to carry out the revisions and corrections which may be necessary on each of these volumes" (*BSJV*, 104:18). Seven works duly came out from 1906 to 1914.

In English, the book first appeared as *Kongre, the Wrecker, or, The Lighthouse at the End of the World* in *The Boy's Own Paper* (October 1914 to September 1915), then in volume form with Sampson Low (1923). Cranstoun Metcalfe's translation, of "relatively good quality,"[21] was praised in the *New York Times* for the "velocity and the variety of [the] narrative."[22] Surprisingly, however, no substantive book review or study of *Lighthouse* has ever been produced in any language.

The inevitably unfaithful Spanish-American film got poor reviews in 1971, although one critic praised the harsh realism (ten minutes were cut for U.S. cinemas). Set partly at night and with a woman added—and raped—Yul Brynner and Kirk Douglas remain the focus of attention as the opposing protagonists.

Thinking about *Lighthouse* has, however, been transformed recently. At a 1978 conference in Cerisy, scholar Piero Gondolo della Riva showed that the posthumous works were not really by Jules Verne, for Michel's revisions and additions were substantial, amounting as much as to two-thirds of each work. His argument was based on the typescripts of five works (not including *Lighthouse*), previously in the possession of Hetzel's heritors. These were very different from the published versions but conformed to the manuscripts owned by Jean Jules-Verne. Three years later the grandson's estate sold the ninety-plus manuscripts to the City of Nantes for six million francs. The Société Jules Verne then published the original, Jules Verne, versions of the five novels (1985–89), reportedly with the approval of Nantes in the case of "Storitz."[23]

Jules's manuscript of *Lighthouse*, which had not been examined closely in the mistaken belief that Michel made few changes, was finally published in 1999.[24] It is this version that appears here for the first time in English.

We now therefore have two versions of the novel, the one entirely by Jules and the one revised by Michel (henceforth: the Michel version), and so can assess their relative value.

The general question of the posthumous alterations has generated a great deal of heat in France. Many critics consider the Michel versions better in significant respects. Heuré (82) points out that the Jules manuscripts are sometimes repetitive and clumsy. In the article that started off the whole debate, Gondolo della Riva (*Europe*) considers that several of the novels published before 1905 lack action and originality, with too many enumerations and digressions, whereas the posthumous works are rich with ideas, due to Michel's intervention. Martin concurs, opining that "the main interest of the [posthumous] novels comes most often from the son's work" (*Jules Verne*, 258). Compère claims that from 1891 Verne had his son, wife, granddaughters, and others copy out his manuscripts and that he collaborated extensively with his son.[25] He postulates that many of the differences between the manuscripts and the posthumous publications were in fact introduced by Verne himself on intermediate versions that have not survived. Above all, he argues, since Verne always revised extensively on proofs, the posthumous text is closer to his intentions than the manuscript version, which represents a mere "first draft." A review of *Magellania* argues that it reads like an outline rather than a polished book, with little happening for the first hundred pages, and too much telling and not enough showing; but that Michel's version, in contrast, although reflecting his own personal views, constitutes a vivid, literary novel with comprehensive development of the many ideological crosscurrents.[26]

However, in a coauthored article of 2000, Gondolo della Riva apparently changes position, now stating that Michel's "revisions often traduce the thinking of the author."[27] Mostly in the *Bulletin* that he himself edits, Dumas has written scores of polemical articles on the posthumous question—"with excessive vehemence," according to the *Extrapolation* review. He strenuously argues that Michel's work on the posthumous volumes was duplicitous and morally reprehensible. In the case of *Lighthouse*, he says the son failed to check the typescript against the manuscript, "weakens" the style, and that nearly all his changes were for the worse.[28] His position is reflected in his title, "Do You Prefer the True or Fake Jules Verne?"[29] Dumas's arguments have greatly influenced recent debate, especially the half-dozen popular biographies that came out for the centenary in 2005.

It might be expected that publishers, with access to expert legal advice and reputations at stake, would have addressed the three-decades-old Jules-Michel question of the posthumous works, if only to reconsider the authorship formula of their books—but such a view overestimates their literary sensibility and speed of reaction.[30] Apart from publishers specifically producing the Jules version, a deafening silence has ensued. Livre de Poche has issued neither edition of the posthumous novels since 1978; and a few publishers—including one of the English *Lighthouse*—are still continuing to issue the Michel version under Jules Verne's sole name, despite the clear untruth and illegality of such an action.

The Michel controversy is, then, still in full flow, in France at least. Most critics have taken on trust Dumas's claim of the literary superiority of Jules's version. However, his arguments have often been one-sided and indeed tendentious, and commentary to date has suffered from lack of a detailed comparison of the two texts. This missing evidence will be adduced here for the first time.

Even Dumas admits that the manuscript of *Lighthouse* needs some revision (*BSJV*, 116:19). In addition to the errors of crossing out and the gaps, there are stylistic tics, such as the overuse of sentences beginning with "and," "and then," "and indeed," or "here is." Some of the paragraph divisions also seem redundant.

Although the text reads well, in the later chapters Verne may perhaps go too far in drawing up hypotheses in elaborate detail, then repeating them, although often the contemplated eventuality never happens. A better balance between creation of anxiety and depiction of gruesome events might sometimes be preferable.

Michel makes few changes in chapters 1 to 3. The remainder of Verne's text sometimes has inappropriate prepositions, lacks continuity, or contains inconsistencies. Michel corrects factual discrepancies, polishes and shortens sentences, improves flow, and cuts repetition. Despite their number, his changes rarely introduce new material; he attempts, the most often successfully, to render the text more concise and coherent. As an indication of his revisions, the significant variants in chapter 4, similar to those of later chapters, will be indicated in the relevant notes (see pp. 155–58).

In later chapters Michel removes Vasquez's tears and appeals to divine aid. He adds an episode of six pages in chapter 13 where Vasquez heroically blows up the schooner's rudder with a cartridge he has invented (p. 127). Finally, he improves the paragraph concluding the book (p. 145).

In ten previous studies of Jules Verne's manuscripts, I have keenly defended the original versions of the novels, since the involvement of Hetzel père often distorted the contents, including the plot and the ideology. But in the case of *Lighthouse*, I consider Michel's interventions different, since they are concerned with consistency, brevity, elegance, and balance, rarely changing the contents. To a large extent, they represent what Jules himself might have done.

In the absolute, we must consider Michel's changes on balance improvements of the book. However, the modern tendency is to restore literary texts to versions before editing by publishers and later generations; and Verne has the moral right for his text to be available. As a result, literary scholars, at least, are obliged to refer to the Jules Verne version. It is hoped the present edition can contribute to the debate on the merits of the two books.

In some ways *Lighthouse* is the writer's *Lost Illusions*. Always a trenchant observer of human society, often mocking humanity's greed and thirst for power, even Verne's earliest works rarely present human endeavor positively, apart from the—quickly exhausted—exploration of new lands. Knowledge for the sake of it, family life, indulgence of the senses, public service, political or social improvement—all values appear skewwhiff in Verne. Science receives short shrift except as a quicker method to transport the characters away from modern civilization. In the later works science has become systematically nefarious; and the pessimism, which had been present since before *Paris in the Twentieth Century* (c. 1863), becomes stronger. After the first great wave of geographical discovery, what is lacking is simply any metaphysical system, any successful transcendence, any explicit vision of what life is about. All Verne's creatures are first cousins to Captain Nemo and Phileas Fogg, unable—or unwilling—to articulate any coherent scheme of things, any overall philosophy. As a result, and according to the definition of modernity as escaping the ideological straitjackets of the century—whether social, political, religious, or academic—the French novelist must be considered to verge on the postmodern. Anyone looking for explicit messages in *Lighthouse* will be disappointed.

What the reader finds instead is a suspense thriller crossed with a desert-island and sea novel. Verne usually inserts an occasional comic scene in his dramatic or tragic works, but light relief is entirely lacking here.

While *Lighthouse* has been called as "desolate and . . . harsh as the landscapes it describes" (Jules-Verne, 211), most critics have praised its readability and ingenious plotting. Some have argued that the story is slight (Evans, 119–20) or that the literary qualities do not reach those of the other works of the period (Dumas, *BSJV*, 116:17). However, others have nothing but praise: Martin lauds "its purity and simplicity," calling it "a very fine novel" ("Préface," 96), and Metcalfe unequivocally defines it as "a little masterpiece."

Those expecting a psychological novel—or a science-fiction one—will, nevertheless, be disappointed. Characters and even action are secondary, and science plays no role. Women are totally and irrevocably absent, apart from the true heroine, the sea. Her perfect companion is the lighthouse, a powerful symbol of the impotence of human technology against the savage elements. Against all the bloodshed and evil, the darkness, death, and despair, the beacon brings only a little light: positive action in a fallen world can at best hold back the dark forces for a while.

Almost as a backdrop to the raging natural forces, two tales of suspense run in parallel: Kongre and Carcante's attempts to escape before the authorities return; and Vasquez and Davis's efforts to stop them. The narration identifies with the intelligent and far-reaching cogitations of each group and ultimately and contradictorily with both. But heroes and villains are kept apart, in both the chapter structure and the flesh. Only at the very end does the camera pan from attackers to attacked, who meet for the first time at the lighthouse—and in death.

Verne's four main characters are relatively well drawn for an adventure story. All are equally determined and energetic, experienced and brave.[31]

Argentine Chief Petty Officer Vasquez, without a Christian name, is forty-seven but still hale and hearty, and inspires confidence as head keeper. Having sailed the seven seas with the Navy and volunteered for the Lighthouse, he wrong-headedly tries to convince his fellow keepers their isolation is not frightening. After the massacre, his sole thought is revenge, with regular appeals to his God, an Old Testament–style one a million miles from Christian ideas of forgiveness or redemption. But God—as distinct from Providence—rarely intervenes in the Extraordinary Journeys; and Vasquez, surviving through his own audacity, has to do all His dirty work for Him.

American John Davis, hailing from Mobile, thirty to thirty-five, ex-Navy, first officer in the Merchant Marine, has an iron temperament. Davis and Vasquez are both passionate and efficacious individuals, working perfectly together, Davis's control and laconicism complementing the Argentine's hot-headedness and occasional sentimentality. Although of superior rank, Davis follows rather than leads, presumably because he is younger and not on home ground.[32]

Kongre, forty, possesses no other name; it is not even clear whether he is European or Indian; a former captain, his first piratical activities were near the Solomons. With wild features and a thick beard, he is a combinatorial genius like Vasquez, a laconic, efficient doer like Davis, courageous, persistent, and loyal like them both—and a violent sociopath, almost in the Lector league in calculating his own naked advantage. At the end, rather than give in, he proudly chooses the absolute gesture.

Chilean Carcante is thirty-five to forty, of unknown family and origin. Of medium height but sinewy, immensely strong and brave, a faithful deputy and a false heart, he similarly stops at nothing.

The titanic struggle between good and evil, between civilization and its enemies, is thus presented here in its most basic, stripped-down form. With cold perseverance and great resourcefulness on both sides, *Lighthouse* resembles a game of chess played by Hong Kong businessmen, endlessly guessing what the opponent might know and doing multivariate probabilistic analysis on the multiply branching courses of action open to them.

Verne's wish, of course, is for civilized behavior and convictions to finally beat human savagery. In other works, he poses a similar question, but distributes good and evil differently. In the Robur novels, light and dark mix and fight within the same great mind. In *Twenty Thousand Leagues* the question is simply how to respond when unjustly attacked. This simultaneously moral and practical question is often avoided by the woolly-minded in safe democracies: what to do when confronted with ruthless adversaries—behave like them or uphold liberal standards?

Lighthouse answers that there is no perfect response, that civilized behavior does not win the day, for two out of three keepers die, together with scores of innocent shipwrecked sailors. Turning the other cheek is never contemplated. Although evil eventually loses all the more, the bleak conclusion is that life is not always fair, there is no universal redemption. But to compensate, Verne's main answer is practical and resounding: you riposte and you seek full revenge and punishment! As a result, there are an unusual number of deaths in this tale (making one wonder what effect it had on the children it was often given to).

With perfect unity of time and place, with fatal wrecks, cruel pirates, and model sailors, *Lighthouse* is the only Extraordinary Journey without a journey. A pagan story of sky, land, and water mixed with wind, wave, and rock, it revels sensually in the tempting cavities, the vertical cliffs, and the climactically tempestuous hurricanes.

In guise of conclusion, it may be best simply to cite Metcalfe's of eighty years ago: *Lighthouse at the End of the World* stands out through the remoteness of its setting, its creation of dramatic dread, the excitement of its race against time. The rest is pure action, courage, and resourcefulness pitted against ferocity and power of numbers. The greatness of Jules Verne, unparalleled master of the adventure story, is perhaps most apparent in his simplest work.

BACKGROUND NOTE ON STATEN ISLAND

Although situated entirely in the Atlantic Ocean, Staten Island (Isla de los Estados) is the last fragment of the Magellanic archipelago, or Magallanes, the culminating point of the Andes mountain range, and the end of the Americas. One of the few uninhabited areas in the world, it lies east of Le Maire Strait, used by the ships doubling Cape Horn and where the world's two greatest oceans clash.

With 73 days of storm a year, 250 inches of precipitation, and a mean temperature of two or three degrees centigrade, snow lies for eight months a year. Mountainous, but with more than a hundred lakes that feed streams and waterfalls, it now forms a nature reserve. The south coast appears particularly desolate and daunting, punished by storms straight from the Pole. Before the Panama Canal opened in 1914, thousands of ships used it en route to Australia, Asia, or the west coast of America, despite the six-knot currents, stormy seas, and frequent fogs, and despite the seven or eight ships wrecked on its shores every year.

Although sometimes considered part of Tierra del Fuego ("Land of Fire"), Verne himself implies it is separate, and therefore also probably from Patagonia, though not from the Magallanes.

The region was discovered by Magellan in 1520 when he sailed through the Strait of Magellan. In 1578 Sir Francis Drake sighted the point baptized Cape Horn in 1616 by Dutchmen Le Maire and Schouten. These two navigators also discovered new land, calling it Staten in honor of the States of Holland. They believed it to be part of a southern continent, but it was circumnavigated in 1643.

Visited by buccaneers including Bartholomew Sharp, Cavendish, Drake, and Hawkins, used as a hiding place over the centuries by gangs operating from the Falklands, Staten Island was visited by James Cook in 1768 and 1774–75. Mooring in Port San Juan, he killed large numbers of sea lions and fur seals for oil, then sailed southeast in search of an elusive Antarctic continent. Many other explorers' names are linked with the island—some because they were wrecked on it.

The sovereignty of the island was indeterminate for most of the nineteenth century. After losing some of her North American colonies in 1776, Britain thought of settlement in the area to support whalers and sealers. In 1792 the Spanish arrived on Staten Island for the first time. Rumors also came that the lost colony of New Ireland had been on Staten. But no systematic exploration or nomenclature was attempted until Philip Parker King in 1826–28 and Robert Fitzroy with the young Charles Darwin in 1831–36. The exploration work was continued by Luis Vernet (1826), Jules Dumont d'Urville (1837), Charles Wilkes (1839), and William Parker Snow (1855). There were no confirmed European settlements in the Magallanes until 1865.

Argentina, independent since 1816, claimed Staten Island as a dependency of the Falklands, and granted the island to Luis Piedra Buena in 1868 (Vairo, xiv), from whom the British unsuccessfully tried to buy half, for wood for the Falklands. The island remained the private property of Buena's heirs until the Argentine government purchased it in 1912.

As late as 1881 a treaty gave Chile possession of most of the Magallanes, with Argentina taking less than half of Tierra del Fuego Island, plus Staten Island. However, the frontier was still so controversial in 1887 that Hetzel fils refused to publish a map showing it.[33]

NOTES

Maps of Staten Island are available in Bronner (inside front and back cover); Miller, 73; Pétel, 206; and Vairo, 21 and 24–25.

1. Letters to Mario Turello of 20 December 1900 and 6 January 1901 (*Europe*, 58 [May 1980], 128). That summer his eyesight was no better: "he can no longer read, no longer write" (*Entretiens*, 156).
2. Jan Feith, "Le Globe-trotter chez lui" [The globetrotter at home], BSJV, 145: 10.
3. *Jules Verne en son temps* [Jules Verne in his time], ed. Jean-Michel Margot (Amiens: Encrage, 2004), 243.
4. Google Earth (earth.google.com) provides a useful topography of the island. Vairo (xiv) indicates many differences between Verne's account, set in 1859, and the historical one of 1884. Verne's Elgor Bay is on the east coast, between Cape San Juan and Several (or Fallows)

Point (Pétel, 209), whereas the historical lighthouse was on the north coast, on the west side of Port San Juan. Verne's choice seems strange, since the northern coast is better for the busy Le Maire Strait. The name Lighthouse at the End of the World seems to have been retrospectively applied to the 1884 beacon after 1905 to benefit from the link with Verne.

5. A second lighthouse was lit in 1902 in a more sensible place on Observatory Island, six miles north of Staten; it is still standing and resembles Verne's, with its cylindrical shape, lookout gallery, and shedlike outhouses. A third was later built at Cape del Medio on the western tip of Staten (Pétel, 209), sometimes called the Le Maire Lighthouse.

Apparently just for its symbolic value, French entrepreneur and publicist André Bronner decided to build a fourth Lighthouse at the End of the World (Dominique Buffier, *Les Archives du Monde*, "Jules Verne l'universel" [The universal Jules Verne] [March 2005], 78). His aim seems to have been to pay homage to Verne, even if both the Cape San Juan location and the shape of the building were different. Apparently linked with Bronner's endeavor, President Jacques Chirac gave President Carlos Menem a copy of the original edition of *Lighthouse* (Michel's) during his official visit to Argentina in 1997. With a budget of three million francs and the support of corporate sponsors, senior politicians, and the Argentine Army, the solar-panel lighthouse was lit in 1998. In 2000 a replica of Bronner's reconstruction—a fifth iteration—was built at Pointe de Minimes, La Rochelle, the nostalgia being increased by the realization that GPS will render lighthouses increasingly obsolescent.

6. Vairo, xiv. The plot of *Lighthouse* also resembles a violent prison riot on Staten Island. When the 1884 lighthouse was decommissioned in 1902, the climate being found too harsh, the island's prison settlements were also abandoned. During the transfer, the eighty-three prisoners mutinied, killing two wardens and all comrades who refused to join them. After manhunts over several months, the ringleaders were executed, although five prisoners remained unaccounted for (Vairo, xiv). However, all this occurred after Verne's first draft, so may be coincidental.

7. Vairo in private correspondence. Gerlache's "Fifteen Months in the Antarctic" (Gallica), with a preface by Elisée Reclus (Brussels: Guy Leprat, 1902), contains a brief description of the area around San Juan.

8. Letter from Verne to Mario Turiello (5 February 1895), reproduced in *Europe* (1936) 2.1: 171–72.

9. "Memories of Childhood and Youth" (1891).

10. *BSJV*, 119: 12–14.

11. In fact, only part of the manuscript seems to have a pencil version below the ink one. The manuscript (reference B 123) was kindly made available by the Municipal Library of Nantes; *BSJV*, 103: 52.

12. As can be seen from the folios on the Musée Jules Verne de Nantes Web site, http://www.arkhenum.fr/bm_nantes/jules_verne/.

13. In the present edition, most of Michel's insertions in the gaps are retained, following the Gallimard Folio edition.

14. The March 1905 exchange of letters has disappeared, but was summarized by Hetzel after Verne's death (*BSJV*, 103: 40; letter of 12 May 1905).

15. Cited by Amazon.com in publicity for *Magellania*. Olivier Dumas, "Les Romans modifiés" [The modified novels], *Cahiers du centre d'études verniennes* 4 (1984), 4, cites a similar description of the importance of Verne's work on proofs.

16. The letter is cited in Charles-Noël Martin, *Jules Verne* (Paris: Michel de l'Ormeraie, 1978), 254.

17. On 1 April, accompanied by Emile Berr, director of the *Figaro*, Michel claims to have "discovered" a number of his father's manuscripts in a drawer (*Entretiens*, 250–52); Jules-Verne (346–47) mistakenly implies that *Lighthouse* was among them.

18. In mid-1905 Michel reported (*Entretiens*, 251) that "last year Jules Verne, tired, had finished another book (probably *Invasion of the Sea*, published in the *MÉR*, 1 Jan.–1 Aug. 1905), received proofs, but had no strength to correct them to the end, so returned them to Hetzel with a note 'Revise that yourself . . . I can't do it any more.'"

19. In several previous letters, Michel had suggested transferring the title "Lighthouse at the End of the World" to the longer manuscript then

entitled "The Magallanes: At the End of the World," as it was "more poetic," using the title "Looters of Wrecks" ("Pilleurs d'épaves") or "The Wreckers" ("Les Naufrageurs") for the shorter work; but Hetzel fils rejected the idea.

20. Dumas, "Les Romans modifiés," 5. The differences have not been studied to date, but extracts from the *MÉR* version of ch. 6 (transcribed by Dumas) are cited in Riegert. These variants are detailed in the relevant notes of the present edition; they mainly remove repetition.

21. Arthur B. Evans, "A Bibliography of Jules Verne's English Translations," *Science Fiction Studies* 32.1 (2005), 105–42. It starts: "Chapter 1. / The Inauguration / The sun was setting behind the hills which bounded the view to the west. The weather was fine. On the other side, over the sea, which to the north-east and east was indistinguishable from the sky, a few tiny clouds reflected the sun's last rays, soon to be extinguished in the shades of the twilight which lasts for a considerable time in this high latitude of the fifty-fifth degree of the southern hemisphere. / At the moment when the upper rim of the solar disc alone remained visible, a gun rang out from on board the despatch-boat *Santa-Fé*, and the flag of the Argentine Republic, unfolding in the breeze, was run up to her peak."

22. "Jules Verne, Master of the Improbable," F. Fraser Bond, 4 January 1925, III 21, review of *Their Island Home, Castaways of the Flag*, and *Lighthouse*.

23. Olivier Dumas, "L'Attrape-nigaud de Michel Verne" [Michel Verne's booby-trap], *BSJV*, 153 (2005), 21–24.

 However, the copyright situation has never been clarified. Some of Verne's descendants attempted to prevent the 1995 publication via the courts, but failed (Dumas, *BSJV*, 153). It is possible, then, that the manuscripts of Verne's published works, including *Lighthouse* and the other posthumous novels, are not protected by copyright.

24. Stanké then L'Archipel, then again in the Gallimard Folio edition (2004).

25. Daniel Compère, *Jules Verne* (Amiens: Encrage, 1996), 61–62.

26. Brian Taves, "Verne, Jules: *Magellania*," *Extrapolation* 43.2 (Summer 2002), 232–34.

27. Piero Gondolo della Riva and Jean-Paul Dekiss, "Aperçus biographiques" [Biographical insights] in *Jules Verne à Dinard* (Dinard: Mairie de Dinard [2000]), 23.

28. *BSJV*, 116: 18; "Le Mystère des romans posthumes" [The mystery of the posthumous novels], *Europe* 83 (2005), 203–7.

29. Olivier Dumas, "Préférez-vous le vrai ou le faux Jules Verne?" [Do you prefer the true or fake Jules Verne?] *BSJV*, 122: 11–15.

30. The first brave pioneer was Acadian, based in Greater China, who published "*Humbug*, by Jules Verne, Revised by Michel Verne" in 1991.

31. The following analyses benefit from Claude Lengrand, *Dictionnaire des "Voyages extraordinaires"* [Dictionary of the Extraordinary Journeys] (Amiens: Encrage, 1998), 153 and 241–42.

32. Verne's Spanish speakers are sometimes considered negatively, especially in the early works. But Americans range over the whole spectrum: from the brilliantly polymathic Cyrus Smith of *The Mysterious Island* via the bloodthirsty but sympathetic Civil War veterans of *From the Earth to the Moon*, the devious but generous Altamont in *Hatteras*, or the credulous denizens of *Humbug: The American Way of Life*, to the megalomaniac capitalists Purchasing the North Pole.

33. Éric Weissenberg, "La Carte refusée de *Deux ans de vacances*" [The refused map of *Two Years' Holiday*] (*BSJV*, 151: 52–55).

BIBLIOGRAPHY

Anon. "Deux éclats blancs au bout du monde" [Two white flashes at the end of the world], *Ouest France*, Hors série "Jules Verne" [2005]: 46–47.

Anon. *Isla de los Estados: Carta Historica, 1:125,000* [Staten Island: Historical map]. Buenos Aires: Zagier & Urruty, n.d.

Bronner, André. *Le Phare du bout du monde* [*Lighthouse at the End of the World*]. Grenoble: Glénat, 1999.

Buffier, Dominique. "Les Associés du bout du monde" [The associates of the end of the world]. *Les Archives du Monde*, "Jules Verne l'universel" [The universal Jules Verne] [March 2005]: 78–79.

Butcher, William. *Jules Verne: The Definitive Biography*. New York: Thunder's Mouth, 2006.

Chéné, Stéphane. "Comparaison entre *Les Indes noires* (1877) et *Le Phare du Bout du Monde* (1904)" [Comparison between *The Black Indies* and *Lighthouse at the End of the World* (1904)]. *JV* [Amiens: Centre de Documentation Jules Verne] 31 (July–September 1994): 16–19.

Dumas, Olivier. "*Le Phare du bout du monde*, premier roman posthume" [*Lighthouse at the End of the World*, first posthumous novel]. BSJV, 116: 16–20.

———. "Nouvel éclairage du *Phare du bout du monde*" [New light on *Lighthouse at the End of the World*]. In Jules Verne, *Le Phare du bout du monde: Version d'origine* [*Lighthouse at the End of the World*, original version] (Montréal: Stanké, 1999): 11–17.

Dusseau, Joëlle. *Jules Verne*. Paris: Perrin, 2005.

Entretiens avec Jules Verne [Interviews with Jules Verne], ed. Daniel Compère and Jean-Michel Margot. Geneva: Slatkine, 1998.

Gondolo della Riva, Piero. "A Propos des œuvres posthumes de Jules Verne" [On the posthmous works of Jules Verne] *Europe* 56 (1978): 73–82.

Heuré, Gilles. "*Le Phare du bout du monde*." *Télérama*, Hors série [Special issue], 2005: 82–83.

Martin, Charles-Noel. "Préface." In Jules Verne, *"Mirifiques Aventures de Maitre Antifer" et "Le Phare du bout du monde"* [*Adventures of Captain Antifer* and *Lighthouse at the End of the World*]. Lausanne: Rencontre, 1971. 7–15.

Metcalfe, Cranstoun. "Translator's Note." In Jules Verne [with Michel Verne], *The Lighthouse at the End of the World*, trans. Cranstoun Metcalfe. New York: G. Howard Watt, 1924. vi–vii.

Miller, Ron. *Extraordinary Voyages: A Reader's Companion to the Works of Jules Verne*. King George, Virginia: Black Cat, 2006.

Pétel, Claude. *Le Tour du monde en quarante ans* [Around the world in forty years]. Villecresnes: Villecresnes reprographie, 1998. II: 206–17.

Riegert, Guy. "Repetita Narratio . . ." [Narrative reprises], BSJV, 79: 16–23.

Riffenburgh, Beau. "Jules Verne and the Conquest of the Polar Regions." *Polar Record* 27 (1991): 273–76.

Vairo, Carlos Pedro. *La Isla de los Estados y el Faro del Fin del Mundo* [Staten Island and the Lighthouse at the End of the World]. Tierra del Fuego: Zagier & Urruty, 1997.

Verne, Jules. *Magellania*, trans. Benjamin Ivry. New York: Welcome Rain Publishers, 2002.

———. *Le Phare du bout du monde*. Montréal: Stanké, 1999; Paris: Gallimard Folio, 2004.

Verne, Jules [with Michel Verne]. *Le Phare du bout du monde*. MÉR 2nd series 22 (1905); Paris: Hetzel, 1905.

———. *The Lighthouse at the End of the World*, trans. Cranstoun Metcalfe. New York: G. Howard Watt, 1924.

Verne, Michel, and Hetzel, Jules, fils. Letters exchanged following the death of Jules Verne. BSJV, 103, esp. 40–55, and 104, esp. 12–13, 17–18, 21, and 24–26.

1828   8 February: birth of Jules Verne on Île Feydeau in Nantes, to lawyer Pierre and Sophie Verne, of distant Scottish descent. Both parents have close links with reactionary milieus and the slave trade. The family moves to Quai Jean-Bart, with a magnificent view of the Loire.

1829–30   Birth of brother Paul, later a naval officer and stockbroker; followed by sisters Anna (1837), Mathilde (1839), and Marie (1842). Jules hears street battles in the July Revolution.

1834–36   Goes to boarding school; the teacher is the widow of a sea captain, whose return she still awaits. The Vernes spend the summers staying with a retired slave-runner uncle in bucolic countryside.

1836–40   Attends École Saint-Stanislas. Performs well in geography, singing, Greek, and Latin. Henceforth the family lives half the year at Chantenay, on the Loire.

1840–46   Petit séminaire de Saint-Donatien, then Collège royal de Nantes. Easily passes *baccalauréat*. Writes short prose pieces and four plays, later to be followed by thirty more.

1847   Studies law; marriage of his first cousin, Caroline Tronson, with whom he has long been in love. Experiences a fruitless passion for Herminie Arnault-Grossetière and writes more than fifty poems, many dedicated to her, as well as an unfinished novel, *Un Prêtre en 1839* [A Priest in 1839].

1848 Moves to Paris. Is present at the July disturbances. In the literary salons meets Dumas père and fils and probably Hugo.

1849 Passes law degree and stays on in Paris.

1850 One-act comedy *Les Pailles rompues* [Broken straws] opens at Dumas's Théâtre historique and is published.

1851 Meets author Jacques Arago and frequents Adrien Talexy's musical salon. Publishes two short stories. Has a first attack of facial paralysis.

1852–55 Becomes secretary of the Théâtre lyrique on little or no pay. Organizes a dining club called The Eleven Bachelors, reciting his love poetry to them. Refuses to take over his father's law practice: "literature above all." Publishes three more stories and the play *Les Châteaux en Californie* [Castles in California] in collaboration. His coauthored operetta *Le Colin-maillard* [Blind man's bluff] is performed. Visits brothels in the theater district.

1856 Goes to a wedding in Amiens and meets Honorine de Viane, a young widow with two daughters.

1857–58 Publishes his first book, *Le Salon de 1857* [The 1857 Salon]. Marries Honorine, becomes a stockjobber, and moves several times.

1859–60 Visits Scotland and England, the first of about twenty visits to the British Isles, and is decisively marked by the experience. Writes *Voyage en Angleterre et en Écosse* [*Backwards to Britain*].

1861   2 July–8 August: Norway and Denmark.

3 August: birth of only child, Michel.

1863   31 January: *Cinq semaines en ballon* [*Five Weeks in a Balloon*] is published by Jules Hetzel but sells poorly. [All year dates indicated are those of beginning of first publication, usually as a serial.]

1864   New one-book contract with Hetzel. Publication of "Edgar Poe et ses oeuvres" ["Edgar Allan Poe and His Works"], *Voyages et aventures du capitaine Hatteras* [*Adventures of Captain Hatteras*], and *Voyage au centre de la Terre* [*Journey to the Center of the Earth*]. *Paris au XXe siècle* [*Paris in the Twentieth Century*] is brutally rejected by the publisher.

1865–66   *De la Terre à la Lune* [*From the Earth to the Moon*], *Les Enfants du capitaine Grant* [*Captain Grant's Children*], and "Les Forceurs de blocus" ["Blockade Runners"]. A new contract specifies two hundred thousand words a year. Acquires a boat, visits Italy with Hetzel, and moves summer residence to the fishing village of Le Crotoy.

1867   *Géographie de la France et de ses colonies* [Geography of France and her colonies]. Goes with brother to Liverpool, thence on the *Great Eastern* to America.

1868   Baptizes a new boat the *Saint-Michel*. Visits London.

1869   *Vingt mille lieues sous les mers* [*Twenty Thousand Leagues under the Seas*] and *Autour de la Lune* [*Round the Moon*]. Rents a house in Amiens.

1870   *Découverte de la Terre* [*Discovery of the Earth*]. Hetzel rejects *L'Oncle Robinson* [Uncle Robinson], an early version of *L'Île mystérieuse* [*The Mysterious Island*]. During the Franco-Prussian War Verne is in the National Guard.

1871   Briefly goes back to the Stock Exchange. Father dies.

1872   *Le Tour du monde en quatre-vingts jours* [*Around the World in Eighty Days*], based on a play with Édouard Cadol, and *Le Pays des fourrures* [*The Fur Country*]. Becomes member of the Académie d'Amiens.

1873–74   *Le Docteur Ox* [*Dr Ox's Experiment and Other Stories*] and *L'Île mystérieuse* [*The Mysterious Island*]. Begins collaboration with Adolphe d'Ennery on highly successful stage adaptations of novels (*Le Tour du monde en 80 jours* [1874], *Les Enfants du capitaine Grant* [1878], and *Michel Strogoff* [1880]). Moves to 44 Boulevard Longueville, Amiens.

1876–77   *Le Chancellor* [*The "Chancellor"*], *Michel Strogoff*, *Hector Servadac*, and *Les Indes noires* [*The Black Indies*]. Buys second and third boat, the *Saint-Michel II* and *Saint-Michel III*. Gives huge fancy-dress ball, but wife falls critically ill. Michel rebels and is sent to a reformatory. Is sued for plagiarism.

1878   *Un Capitaine de quinze ans* [*The Boy Captain*]. Sails to Portugal and Algeria.

1879–80   *Les Tribulations d'un Chinois en Chine* [*The Tribulations of a Chinese in China*] and *La Maison à vapeur* [*The Steam House*]. Sails to Edinburgh, and then by train and ferry to the Hebrides. Probably has an affair with Luise Teutsch.

1881   *La Jangada* [*The Giant Raft*]. Sails to Holland and Denmark.

1882   *Le Rayon vert* [*The Green Ray*] and *L'École des Robinsons* [*The School for Robinsons*]. Rents a larger house at 2 Rue Charles-Dubois.

1883–84   *Kéraban-le-têtu* [*Keraban the Inflexible*]. Michel marries, but soon abducts a minor, and will have two children by her within eleven months. Verne takes his wife on a grand tour of the Mediterranean, including a private audience with Pope Leo XIII.

1885 *Mathias Sandorf.* Sells *Saint-Michel III.*

1886 *Robur-le-conquérant* [*Clipper of the Clouds*].

9 March: his favourite nephew, Gaston, mentally ill, premeditatedly attempts to murder Verne, laming him for life.

17 March: Hetzel dies.

1887 Mother dies. *Nord contre sud* [*North against South*].

1888 *Deux ans de vacances* [*Two Years' Holiday*]. Elected local councilor on a Republican list. For next fifteen years attends council meetings, administers theater and fairs, and gives public talks.

1889 *Sans dessus dessous* [*Topsy-Turvy*] and "In the Year 2889" (by Michel but signed Jules Verne).

1890 Stomach problems.

1892 *Le Château des Carpathes* [*Carpathian Castle*]. Pays debts for Michel.

1895 *L'Île à hélice* [*Propeller Island*], the first European novel in the present tense and third person.

1896–97 *Face au drapeau* [*For the Flag*] and *Le Sphinx des glaces* [*An Antarctic Mystery*]. Is sued for libel by chemist Turpin. Health deteriorates. Brother dies.

1899 Dreyfus Affair: Verne is anti-Dreyfusard.

1901 *Le Village aérien* [*Treetop Village*]. Moves back to 44 Boulevard Longueville.

1904 *Maître du monde* [*Master of the World*].

1905 17 March: falls ill from diabetes.

24 March: dies. The French government shuns the funeral.

1905–14 On Verne's death, *L'Invasion de la mer* [*Invasion of the Sea*] is in the course of publication. Michel takes responsibility for the manuscripts, publishing *Le Phare du bout du monde* [*Lighthouse at the End of the World,* 1905], *Le Volcan d'or* [*The Golden Volcano*] (1906), *L'Agence Thompson and C°* [*The Thompson Travel Agency*] (1907), *La Chasse au météore* [*The Hunt for the Meteor*] (1908), *Le Pilote du Danube* [*The Danube Pilot*] (1908), *Les Naufragés du "Jonathan"* [*The Survivors of the "Jonathan"*] (1909), *Le Secret de Wilhelm Storitz* [*The Secret of Wilhelm Storitz*] (1910), *Hier et Demain* [*Yesterday and Tomorrow*]—short stories, including "L'Éternel Adam" ["Edom"] (1910), and *L'Étonnante aventure de la mission Barsac* [*The Barsac Mission*] (1914). Between 1985 and 1998 Jules's original versions are published, under the same titles except for *En Magellanie* [*Magellania*], "Voyage d'études" [Study visit], and *Le Beau Danube jaune* [The beautiful yellow danube].

1978   For the 150th anniversary of his birth, the novelist undergoes a major reevaluation in France through hundreds of articles, dissertations, and books. On a cumulative basis, he is the most translated writer of all time.

1989–94   *Voyage à reculons en Angleterre et en Ecosse* [*Backwards to Britain*], *San Carlos et autres récits inédits* [San Carlos and other stories], and *Paris au XXᵉ siècle* [*Paris in the Twentieth Century*], setting a U.S. record for a French book.

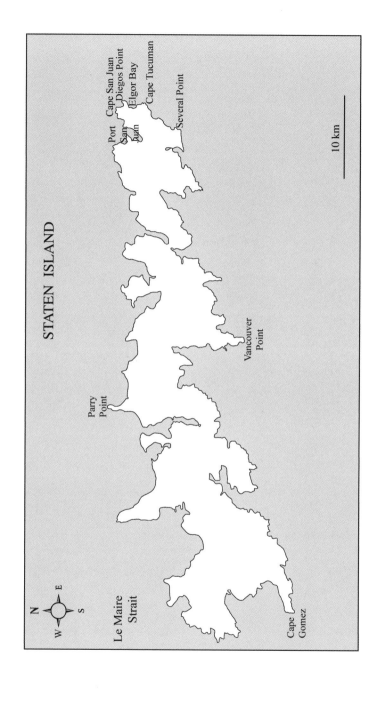

1. Inauguration

The sun was about to sink below the line where sea and sky met, four or five leagues to the west.* The weather was fine. To the east, a scattering of small clouds absorbed the last rays, that would soon fade in the long high-latitude twilight, fifty-five degrees south of the equator.

The solar disc was only half-visible when a cannon sounded aboard the *Santa Fe*.* The flag of the Argentine Republic unfurled in the wind and rose to the head of the sloop's mainmast.

At the same instant a bright light broke from the lighthouse, a gunshot distance behind the narrows of Elgor Bay,* where the *Santa Fe* lay at anchor. Two of the lighthouse keepers, together with the workmen on the beach and the crew assembled on the foredeck, greeted with long cheers the first light to shine out from this remote coast.

Two more cannon shots answered, their detonations reproduced several times by the loud echoes. The sloop struck her colors in accordance with the rules governing warships. And Staten Island,* where the waters of the Atlantic meet the Pacific, fell silent once more.

The workmen quickly boarded the *Santa Fe*, where they would spend this final night, leaving the two keepers alone on shore, for the third remained aloft at his post.

They did not go back to their lodgings, but chatted while strolling along the bay.

"Well, Vasquez!" said the younger one. "Tomorrow the sloop's setting off—"

"Yes, Felipe, I hope her voyage home goes smoothly."

"It's a long way."

"No longer than getting here."

"You don't say," Felipe shot back, amused at his comrade's answer.

"Well, my lad," said Vasquez, "sometimes it *does* take longer to get there than to come home. Unless the wind helps you along, that is. Fifteen hundred miles is nothing with a good engine and a good wind."

"And Captain Lafayate* knows the way like the back of his hand."

"And a direct route it is, lad. He sailed south to come here, and he'll sail north to get back. And if that wind keeps seaward, he'll have the coast for shelter. He might as well be sailing a river, like the Rio de la Plata."

"But a river with only one bank."

"Who cares, as long as you've got a good wind? And it's a good one when it's behind you!"

Vasquez was obviously enjoying the cheerful repartee with his colleague, who now came back with "Right! But what if the wind turns around?"

"That, Felipe, would be bad luck, which is one thing I hope the *Santa Fe* won't have. She could do her fifteen hundred miles and be anchored in Buenos Aires in a fortnight. Now if the wind veered westerly—"

"There'd be no port to shelter in. Neither on land nor on water."

"As you say, lad. There's not a port in the whole of Tierra del Fuego or Patagonia.* Not one. So if they don't want to hit dry land, they'd better hit the high seas!"

"But actually, Vasquez, the weather looks as though it'll hold."

"I think so, Felipe. We're coming into the fine season. Three great months—that's really something."

"They finished work at just the right time."

"I know, lad, I know. Early December here is what northern sailors would call early June. Of course there's the squalls that'll think nothing of sinking a ship as easy as whipping your sou'wester off. But they don't happen all that often. And once the *Santa Fe*'s in port, the storms can rage as much as the devil wants! No fear, our island's not going to topple into the deep, lighthouse and all!"

"Hopefully, Vasquez. Anyway, when they bring news from home and come back with the relief team—"

"In three months, Felipe."

"Yes—three months! But this island won't go anywhere in that time."

"Nor will we," replied Vasquez, rubbing his hands. He had just taken a long puff of his pipe and thick smoke surrounded him. "See here, lad, this isn't like being aboard some boat, rocked back and forth by the storm. Or say this *is* a boat, moored to the tail of America, and she's not going to drag anchor! Not that these aren't rough waters. It's only fair to say the Cape Horn seas are ill-famed.* Why, a man couldn't even count the number of wrecks on these coasts!* A looter couldn't find a better place to make his fortune. But that's all going to change, Felipe. Staten Island has a lighthouse now. All the hurricanes from every corner of the horizon couldn't blow it out; ships'll see it and they'll have time to change course, with the beacon to guide them. No danger of running onto those rocks at Cape Tucuman or Several Point.* Not even when you can't see your hand in front of your face. We're the ones to keep the lantern shining, and we'll do it properly!"

Vasquez's tone of conviction touched Felipe. Perhaps the latter did not feel quite as lighthearted about the long weeks he would be spending on this deserted island, cut off from humanity until the trio were relieved. But this aspect did not seem to bother Vasquez, for he concluded:

"See here, lad. I've spent these forty years sailing every sea in the Old World and New. I've been cabin boy, midshipman, sailor, and officer. Well now that I'm getting on, I couldn't hope for better than keeping a lighthouse. And not just any—the Lighthouse at the End of the World!"

And at the tip of this forsaken island, at the limit of inhabited and inhabitable lands, the name was apt.

"Say, Felipe," added Vasquez. His pipe had gone out and he was tapping it on his hand. "When d'you relieve Moriz?"

"At ten. Until two in the morning."

"Good. After that it's me on until first light."

"So the most sensible thing is for us to get some sleep!"

"To bed, then, Felipe. To bed!"

Vasquez and Felipe went up to the little perimeter around the lighthouse, and into the living quarters. The door closed behind them.

They spent a peaceful night. Vasquez concluded it by putting out the light, which had been burning for twelve hours.

The tide is not usually strong in the vast Pacific, especially along the American and Asian coasts. But Atlantic tides are vigorous, and their force is felt even on the most distant shores of the Magallanes.*

The sea began going out at six in the morning.* If the sloop had wanted to take advantage of the tide, she would have needed to sail at daybreak. But she was not quite ready and so the captain planned to leave Elgor Bay on the evening tide.

The *Santa Fe*, of the Argentine Navy, was of 200 tons' burden and 160 horsepower. Her captain and first officer headed a crew of about fifty, including the petty officers. She had been assigned to coastal patrol from the mouth of the Rio de la Plata to Le Maire Strait* on the Atlantic Ocean. Marine engineering had not yet designed cruisers, torpedo-boats, and other fast ships, and the *Santa Fe*'s propeller gave her a speed of only nine knots. But that would do for policing the coasts of Patagonia and Tierra del Fuego, frequented only by fishing boats.

That year,* the government of Argentina was building a lighthouse on Staten Island, at the mouth of Le Maire Strait, and had detailed the *Santa Fe* to transporting the men and equipment for construction. They had followed the plans of a skilled Buenos Aires engineer and the lighthouse was now finished.

The *Santa Fe* had been moored at the end of Elgor Bay for about three weeks. After unloading four months of provisions, and so ensuring the new lighthouse keepers would have plenty of supplies until the relief came, Captain Lafayate would take the construction workmen back on board. Had there not been an unexpected delay in completing the work, the *Santa Fe* would have returned to her home port a month earlier.

Captain Lafayate had no reason to worry. His anchorage at the end of the bay was sheltered from northerlies, southerlies, and westerlies. Only bad weather from the open sea could have caused him problems, but at the beginning of summer he was hopeful that the Magellanic waters would see merely brief disturbances.

It was seven o'clock when the captain and First Officer Riegal left their cabins in the wings of the poop, at the aft end of the ship. The sailors had almost finished scrubbing the deck and were pushing the last of the water down through the scupper. The sloop would not be sailing until afternoon, but the chief petty officer was already making preparations as he saw to the removal of the sailcovers, the polishing of the brasswork around the air shafts, binnacles, and deck lights, and the securing of the longboat, leaving the smaller boat available for use. At sunrise the colors were hoisted on the brigantine. Three-quarters of an hour later, four bells sounded for'ard, and the sailors proceeded to their duties.

After a shared breakfast, the two officers returned to the poop to observe the atmospheric conditions, which were fairly good, since the wind was landward. Then they instructed the petty officer to set them ashore.

The captain's agenda that morning was to make one final inspection of the lighthouse and its annexes—the keepers' quarters and the storerooms containing the provisions and fuel—ascertaining that all was in order. Accordingly he and the first officer went ashore. As they made their way to the lighthouse perimeter, they spoke of the three men who would remain in the sad solitude of Staten Island.

"This is a hard assignment," said the captain. "Operating a lighthouse is not easy work, even when in daily contact with the land, not the case here. Of course we have to remember these are good men, used to a tough life. Two of them are former sailors."

"Absolutely," replied Riegal. "But it's one thing to be a lighthouse keeper on a busy coast, and quite another to live on a deserted island where ships never put in. The only reason they sight this island is to give it the widest possible berth."

"Admittedly, Riegal. That's why we'll relieve Vasquez, Felipe, and Moriz in three months. And this is the best season for them to start such an assignment."

"Yes, sir. They'll be spared those terrible Cape Horn winters."

"Terrible, yes. When we did a little reconnaissance in the strait a few years ago, from Tierra del Fuego to Tierra de la Desolacion, between Cape Virgins and Cape Pilar,* I got to know those tempests by heart. But after all, the keepers do have a solid house, and no storm is going to blow it down. They'll have plenty of food and coal even if their term of duty over-runs by two months. We're leaving them in good health, and they'll be in good health when we see them again. Even if the air seems cold, at least it's clean at this entrance to the Atlantic and the Pacific! And there's something else, Riegal: when the Maritime Authority asked for volunteers to run the Lighthouse at the End of the World, the only problem was how to choose."

The two officers had just reached the perimeter, where Vasquez and his colleagues were waiting for them. The gate opened for them and they paused, returning the trio's salutes.

Captain Lafayate studied the three men, from their feet in heavy sea boots to their waxed hoods, and then he spoke.

"Was everything in order last night?"

"Everything, captain," replied Vasquez.

"No ships sighted to sea?"

"None, sir."

"Nor in Le Maire Strait?"

"Nor there, sir. And the sky was clear. We would have seen a light at least four miles away."

"Did the lamps function properly?"

"Yes, sir. From sunset to sunrise."

"Was it cold in the duty room?"

"No, sir. Not a draught. The double glazing keeps the wind out."*

"We will take a look at the living quarters, and then the lighthouse."

"Aye-aye, sir."

Below the tower, the thick walls of the quarters could resist any Magellanic gusts of wind. The two officers visited the well-appointed rooms, safe from rain, cold, and snowstorms, which can be formidable at an almost Antarctic latitude.

A central corridor led to a gate to the tower.

"Let's go up," said Captain Lafayate.

"Aye-aye, sir."

"Only you need come."

Vasquez made a sign to his colleagues to stay at the end of the corridor. Then he opened the gate and the two officers followed him up. The narrow spiral, with stone steps set solidly in the walls, was bright, for a loophole lit each floor.

Reaching the duty room, one level below the lantern and apparatus, the two officers sat on a circular bench running round the wall. The entire horizon was visible through the four small windows.

The wind was moderate, but blew quite strongly at this height, mixed in with the sharp cries of seagulls, frigate birds, and albatrosses, which flew by on powerful wing strokes.

Captain Lafayate and his first officer positioned themselves in front of each window, checking it was in good condition. Then, for a better view of the island and surrounding sea, they climbed the ladder to the gallery around the lantern.

The part of the island stretching westwards before their eyes was as deserted as the sea to the east and south. Equally deserted lay the strait to the north, too wide for its northern shore to be seen. At the foot of the tower curved Elgor Bay, busy with the sailors' comings and goings, as well as the *Santa Fe* at anchor. Not a single sail or smokestack visible to sea. Nothing but the oceanic immensity!

After quarter of an hour on the lighthouse gallery, the two officers, followed by Vasquez, went down again and returned to their ship.

After lunch, Captain Lafayate and First Officer Riegal were set ashore once more. The hours before setting sail would be devoted to a walk along the left bank of Elgor Bay. Several times, and without a pilot—for it will be appreciated there were none on Staten Island—the captain had sailed in daylight to his usual mooring in the little inlet at the foot of the lighthouse. But he always took the precaution of carrying out a reconnaissance.

So the two officers studied certain seamarks as they strolled. Sailing presented no difficulties here if one took care. The depth sufficed for a vessel like the *Santa Fe* anywhere in the bay, even at low tide. And now, thanks to the lighthouse, the bay would be easily navigable at night.

"What a pity," said the captain, "that the approaches to this bay are so dangerous, with all those reefs stretching so far out to sea!

Otherwise, ships in distress could anchor here. Remember, there's nothing else after the Strait of Magellan."*

What he said was only too true. But it will be a long time before a chart shows a harbor at the end of Elgor Bay, on the east coast of Staten Island!

At four o'clock the two officers took leave of Vasquez, Felipe, and Moriz and went back on board. The three stayed on shore in preparation for the ship's departure.

At five o'clock pressure rose in the sloop's boiler as she belched forth whirlwinds of black smoke. The tide would soon be turning, and as soon as it began to descend, the *Santa Fe* would be weighing anchor.

At five forty-five the captain gave orders to heave the capstan. The screw was ready and steam leaked from the pipes.

At the bow the first officer monitored operations; the anchor was soon apeak and secured in the cathead.

The *Santa Fe* got under way, to the farewells of the three lighthouse keepers. Whatever Vasquez's thoughts, and whatever his comrades' feelings as they watched the sloop depart, her officers and crew felt deeply for the three men they were leaving on this island at the tip of America.

The *Santa Fe* took her time as she followed the curves of Elgor Bay. Shortly before eight o'clock she reached the open sea. Rounding Cape San Juan,* she sailed at full steam into the strait. When night fell, the beacon from the Lighthouse at the End of the World had faded to a star, grazing the horizon.*

2. Staten Island

Staten Island—also called Staten Land*—is situated at the south-eastern tip of the New World. It is the last morsel of the Magellanic archipelago, which the convulsions of the plutonian era cast on the waters of the fifty-fifth parallel, less than seven degrees from the Southern Polar Circle.* Bathing in the waters of two oceans, it is sought out by ships passing from one to the other, whether coming from the northeast, or from the southwest after rounding Cape Horn.

Le Maire Strait, discovered in the seventeenth century by the Dutch navigator of that name,* separates Staten Island from Tierra del Fuego, fifteen miles away. It affords vessels a shorter and easier route, allowing them to avoid the formidable swells of the dangerous seas further east. Staten Island constitutes the southern shore of the strait for about thirty-nine miles,* during which steam and sailing ships are less exposed than when passing south of the island. In other words, Staten Island measures about thirty-nine miles from Cape Gomez in the west to Cape San Juan in the east, by eleven miles from Parry Point to Vancouver Point.*

In geometric terms, this island looks a little like a crustacean. The tip of the creature's tail would be Cape Gomez, and its mouth, Elgor Bay, with Cape Tucuman and Diegos Point* as the lower and upper jaws.

The shore of Staten Island is completely broken up.* It contains a succession of narrow, inaccessible inlets, strewn with reefs sometimes stretching a mile out to sea. Refuge is impossible here from the squalls of the south or north. Fishing smacks could hardly take shelter in the inlets. As a result wreck after wreck has happened on these coasts, here lined with sheer cliffs, there fringed with enormous boulders, against which the sea, excited by the long swells from the deep, crashes with unsurpassed fury, even in calm weather.

The island was at that time uninhabited, but perhaps not uninhabitable, at least in the summer, which at this high latitude comprises November, December, January, and February. Herds would even have found sufficient food on the broad plains stretching into the interior, especially between Parry and Vancouver Points. When the thick coat of snow has melted in the Antarctic sun, the grass appears quite green and the soil retains a healthy amount of moisture until the winter. Ruminants accustomed to the conditions of the Magellanic lands might prosper here. In the cold weather, however, the herds would have to return to the milder climes of Patagonia, if not of Tierra del Fuego.

Nevertheless, there could be found in the wild a few pairs of those guanacos,* a sort of very rustic deer, whose flesh is quite good when suitably roasted or grilled. And if those animals do not die of starvation in the long winter, it is because they are able to fill their stomachs with roots and moss from under the snow.

In addition to the plains stretching inland, a few clumps of trees, spreading their thin branches and bowers, display a short-lived foliage, more yellowish than verdant. These are mainly Antarctic beeches, sometimes more than sixty feet tall, whose branches ramify horizontally. There is also a very tough variety of barberry called Winter's bark, having more or less the properties of cinnamon.*

In actual fact, the plains and woods cover less than a tenth of Staten Island. The rest is composed of rocky, quartz-based plateaus, deep gorges, and long trails of blocks erratically scattered by age-old eruptions, although one would search in vain at the present day for the craters of extinct volcanoes in this Fuegian or Magellanic region. Among the plateaus there are even very broad ones which look like steppes when covered with coats of snow for the eight winter months, without even bulges to break up the monotony. Then, as one heads west, the relief of the island becomes more accentuated and the shoreline cliffs higher and steeper. There stand haughty cones, peaks of considerable stature, reaching three thousand feet above sea level and affording a view of the whole island. These are the last links of the prodigious Andean chain that runs the entire length of the New World.

Certainly, in such weather conditions, in the breath of the biting, terrible hurricanes, the island's flora merely comprises a few rare specimens. They belong to species generally only acclimatized to the area around the Strait of Magellan or the Falklands Archipelago, about a hundred leagues from the Fuegian coast: calceolarias, laburnums, burnets, bromes, speedwells, and feather-grasses,* none of which possesses very much coloring at all. Under the cover of the woods, among the prairie grasses, these pale florets display their half-faded petals, which disappear almost straightaway. At the foot of the coastal rocks, on the slopes where a little soil clings, naturalists might still gather some varieties of moss; under the trees they could also find a few edible roots, namely those of an azalea, which the Pécherais* use for a rather unnourishing bread.

Besides, one would search in vain for a permanent watercourse on Staten Island. Neither stream nor brook springs from this stony ground. But the snow gathers in thick layers; it lies eight months out of twelve, and in the warm season—less cold would be more accurate—it melts in the oblique rays of the sun, maintaining constant moisture. Ponds and pools form here and there, whose water lies in turn until the first frosts. This was why quantities of water were falling from the heights behind the lighthouse, running down to disappear in the little inlet of Elgor Bay.

If fauna and flora are hardly present on the island, fish in contrast abound along the whole coast: despite the great danger of crossing Le Maire Strait, the Fuegians* sometimes sail here for abundant catches. A multitude of species teem: hake, hammerheads, smelts,* loaches, skipjacks, sea bream, gobies, and mullet. And bigger prey could even bring in numerous ships, for cetaceans often frequented these waters, cachalots and other whales as well as seals and walruses, at that time at least. The truth is that such creatures have now been hunted down with such lack of foresight that they take refuge in the Antarctic seas, where campaigns are both dangerous and difficult.

It will easily be understood that the whole island perimeter, with its succession of beaches, coves, and rocky banks, abounds with shells and shellfish: bivalves and others, mussels, winkles, oysters, *Fissurella*, other limpets, and whelks, with thousands of crustaceans threading their way through the reefs.

As for the avian class, it is represented by countless albatrosses as white as swans, snipe, plovers, sandpipers, sea larks, noisy gulls of every variety, and deafening skuas.

But it should not be concluded from this description that Staten Island was of a nature to excite the rapacity of Chile or the Argentine Republic. It was after all just a rock, albeit an enormous one, and more or less uninhabitable. Who did it belong to when this story began? All that can be said is that it formed part of the Magellanic archipelago, which had not at that time been divided between the two republics of the tip of the American continent.*

In the fine season, Fuegians, or Pécherais, make rare appearances when heavy weather forces them to put in. In any case, apart from Elgor Bay, at that time little known, the island offers no haven to steam or sailing vessels following Le Maire Strait or passing to the south. Also, with the progress of steam navigation, the majority of ships, whether coming from the east or west, prefer to sail from one ocean to the other via the Strait of Magellan, charted with extreme precision. The only ships that come into contact with Staten Island are those preparing to double redoubtable Cape Horn or those that have just doubled it.

It should be pointed out that the Argentine Republic took a worthy initiative when it constructed this Lighthouse at the End of the World, for which other countries should be grateful. Previously no light shone over these Magellanic regions, none for the whole passage from the Atlantic entrance of the Strait of Magellan at Cape Virgins to its exit at Cape Pilar on the Pacific. The Staten Island lighthouse was about to render indisputable service to navigation on these dangerous waters. Even at Cape Horn there is not a single lighthouse, although it would prevent many disasters. Such a sorely needed beacon would ensure greater safety both for ships entering Le Maire Strait only to risk the reefs of Cape San Juan, and for those rounding Several Point and passing below the island.

The Argentine government had, then, decided to build a new lighthouse, and the position it chose was the end of Elgor Bay.* After a year of well-executed work, the structure had just been inaugurated on this 9 December 1859.*

Fifty meters away from the small inlet at the far end of the bay, a flattish outcrop, approximately ten meters high, covered four or five hundred square meters.* A dry-stone wall enclosed this platform, the rocky terrace which served as foundation for the lighthouse tower.

The latter rose centrally above the annex complex, made up of living quarters and storerooms.

More precisely, the annex* consisted of:

1. the keepers' bedroom, with beds, wardrobes, tables, and chairs, heated by a coal stove with a chimney to evacuate the smoke;

2. the common room, also heated, which served as dining room, with a table in the center, hanging ceiling lamps, cupboards containing instruments such as telescopes, barometers, thermometers, and

the lamps designed to replace the main lantern in case of accident, as well as a grandfather clock, standing against the side wall;

3. storerooms containing six months of provisions, although new supplies and a relief team would come every three months: preserves of every sort, salt meat, corned beef, bacon, dried vegetables, sea biscuits, tea, coffee, sugar, and kegs of whiskey and brandy, to be diluted with water from the inlet at the foot of the terrace when the snow melted, plus a few common medical items;

4. the stocks of oil for the lighthouse lamps;

5. the fuel store, with sufficient quantities of coal for the keepers for the whole Antarctic winter.

Such was the complex of buildings on the terrace, forming a more or less circular structure.

The tower was built extremely solidly, using materials from Staten Island itself. Its granite-hard stone, aligned with great precision, interlocking, dovetailing, and locked in position with metal braces, formed a barrier able to resist cruel storms, the terrible hurricanes which raged so frequently on this distant meeting place of the globe's two greatest oceans. As Vasquez said, the wind would not destroy this tower. It would be a beacon he and his comrades intended to maintain, maintain well despite the Magellanic tempests!

The tower stood thirty-two meters high and, adding the height of the terrace, its light shone 126 feet above sea level. It could therefore in theory be seen ten miles out to sea, although in practice its range was limited to eight miles.*

At that time lighthouses operating with hydrocarbon gas did not exist, nor those using electricity. In any case, oil lighting was the only option on that faraway island, difficult to reach even from the closest nations. Accordingly oil was used, while including all the improvements that science and industry had made until then.

In fact, this range of ten miles was enough for ships, whether coming from the east, northeast, or southeast. They still had a wide berth for either reaching Le Maire Strait or else heading south of the island. All danger would be obviated by scrupulously observing the directives of the Maritime Authority: keep the lighthouse to north-northwest in the former case, or to south-southwest in the latter.* Cape San Juan and Several Point would be cleared by passing respectively to port or starboard, in time to avoid being embayed by the wind or currents.

In addition, on the very rare occasions when a vessel was forced to anchor in Elgor Bay, she would have every chance of reaching her mooring by following the lighthouse. When she came back, the *Santa Fe* could thus easily head for the little inlet at the end of the bay, even at night. Since the bay was about three miles long and the range of the beam eight miles, the sloop would still have five to spare before hitting the reefs of the island.

Previously, lighthouses had been equipped with parabolic mirrors, which had the serious disadvantage of absorbing at least half the light produced. But progress had occurred in this area as in all others. Dioptric mirrors were now used which wasted only a small part of the light from the lamps.

It goes without saying that the Lighthouse at the End of the World had a fixed beam. There was no danger a ship's captain would confuse it with another, since none existed in this region, not even, it should be repeated, on Cape Horn. There seemed little point consequently in distinguishing it by using intermittences or flashes, thus allowing the omission of a delicate mechanism, always difficult to repair on an island inhabited only by three keepers.

The lantern was equipped with lamps with double air inlets and concentric lenses.* Their flames produced an intense light in a small space, and hence could be brought very close to the focus of the lenses. Plenty of oil reached them using a system similar to the Carcels'.* As for the dioptric system of the lantern, it was made up of layered lenses, consisting of a central glass of ordinary shape, with a series of thin rings all having the same focus. Thanks to their annular tambour shape, they met all the demands of a system with a fixed light. The lenses produced a cylindrical beam of parallel rays which carried, in optimal visibility, a distance of eight miles. By leaving the island in fine weather, the sloop's captain could check that no adjustment was needed in the design or operation of the new lighthouse.

It was clear that proper functioning depended on the meticulousness and vigilance of the keepers. Provided they kept the lamps in perfect order, carefully replaced the wicks, ensured the required amounts of oil were available, adjusted the focal distance by lengthening or shortening the rod covers of the glasses,* lit and extinguished the light at sunset and sunrise, in sum maintained a scrupulous and constant supervision, this lighthouse would render tremendous service to navigators on these far waters of the Atlantic Ocean.

There was in fact no reason to doubt the good will and steady zeal of Vasquez and his two colleagues.

It is appropriate to recall that the security of the three keepers seemed to be assured, so isolated was Staten Island, fifteen hundred miles from Buenos Aires, the only port from which provisioning and help could come. The few Fuegians and Pécherais who came over in the fine season never spent long here. Their fishing finished, they were in a hurry to recross Le Maire Strait and head back to Tierra del Fuego or the surrounding islands. Never in the past had strangers been observed. The island's coasts were so difficult that navigators tempted to seek shelter here would in fact find safer and easier refuge at several other points of the Magallanes.

However, every precaution had been taken in case dubious characters did arrive at Elgor Bay. The annexes had solid doors that bolted from the inside, and the bars on the storeroom and quarters windows could never be forced. In addition Vasquez, Moriz, and Felipe possessed rifles and revolvers with plenty of ammunition.

Finally, at the end of the corridor which led to the foot of the tower, an iron gate had been installed, impossible to break or bend. As for entering the tower some other way, how could the loopholes of the staircase be used, protected as they were by solid crossbars; and how could the gallery surrounding the lantern be reached without climbing up the cable of the lightning conductor?*

Such were the extensive works which had just been completed on Staten Island, thanks to the efforts of the government of the Argentine Republic.

3. The Three Keepers

It is at this time of year, from November to March, that most navigation takes place in the waters of the Magallanes. The sea is always difficult there. But if nothing stops or calms the huge swells that come from the two oceans, at least the atmospheric conditions change less and the storms which trouble even the upper air do not last long. In this period of moderate weather, steamships and sailing ships more willingly venture* round the new continent by doubling Cape Horn.

And yet the passage of ships through Le Maire Strait or south of Staten Island would not break the monotony of the long days of the season in question. (Vessels were never numerous, and became rarer when the development of steam navigation and the improvement of marine charts made it less dangerous to enter the Strait of Magellan, both the shortest and the easiest route.)

However, this monotony is never such as to upset keepers detailed to running the various lighthouses. They are mostly former sailors or fishermen, and not men to count the days or hours. They are used to keeping themselves busy and amused. Their duties in any case do not consist only of ensuring the light shines from sunset to sunrise.

Vasquez and his colleagues were to carefully monitor the approaches to Elgor Bay, to visit Cape San Juan several times a week, and to observe the east coast from Diegos Point to Several Point, but without ever venturing more than three or four miles away. They had to keep the lighthouse logbook up to date, noting any incident which might occur, the passage of steam or sailing ships, their nationalities, their names when they sent them with their numbers, and finally the height of the tides, the direction and strength of the wind, the weather, the duration of the rain, the frequency of the storms, the rise and fall in the barometer, the temperature, and other phenomena which would allow the meteorological chart of these areas to be drawn.

Vasquez, Argentine by birth like Felipe and Moriz, was to be head lighthouse keeper on Staten Island. He was forty-seven. Vigorous and healthy enough to withstand anything, with a remarkable endurance from his life as a sailor at all latitudes, resolute, energetic, and used to danger, he had managed to get out of several situations where his life had been in danger. It was not only his age that led to his leadership, but his robust character, which inspired complete confidence. Although he had got no higher than chief petty officer in the Navy of the Republic, he had left the service with universal esteem. Accordingly, when he applied to work on Staten Island, the Maritime Authority did not think twice about giving him the position.

Felipe and Moriz, respectively aged forty and thirty-seven, had also been sailors. Vasquez had known their families for many years and had put forward their names. If Felipe also remained a bachelor, Moriz was the only one of the three to be married but had no children. His wife, whom he would see again in three months, worked in a boarding house in the port area of Buenos Aires.

When the three months were up, Vasquez, Felipe, and Moriz would reembark on the *Santa Fe* bringing three new keepers to Staten Island, whose place they would take once more three months later.

It would be in June, July, and August that they would work again, in the depth of winter. In other words, not having suffered too much from bad weather on their first sojourn, they were due for some terrible tempests on returning to the island. But that seemed unlikely to cause them much worry. Vasquez and his colleagues would already be near-acclimatized and able to face the cold, storms, and other rigors of the Antarctic seasons with equanimity.

Starting from that day, 10 December, the work was carefully organized. Each night the lamps operated under the surveillance of one of the keepers in the duty room, while the other two rested in the quarters until due to replace him. During the day they inspected and cleaned the apparatus, fitting it with new wicks if necessary, and generally prepared it for projecting its powerful rays the moment the sun went down.

In between, following the service guidelines, Vasquez and his colleagues would follow Elgor Bay down to the sea either on foot along one of the banks or in the boat left for the keepers, a half-deck launch rigged with a foresail and jib. The boat sheltered in the little inlet, where there was no danger, as high cliffs protected it from the easterlies, the only dangerous winds.

It goes without saying that when Vasquez, Felipe, or Moriz made excursions to the bay or the area around the enclosure, one of them always remained on watch in the gallery at the top of the lighthouse, as a ship might come into view at any time and wish to send her number. From the terrace, the sea could not be seen even eastwards, and to the north and south the cliffs limited the perspective to several hundred meters from the perimeter wall—hence this obligation for one of the keepers to remain permanently in the duty room so as to be able to communicate with ships.

No incident marked the days that followed the departure of the sloop. The weather remained fairly good, the temperature relatively high. The thermometer sometimes read ten degrees centigrade above zero.* The wind blew from the sea, generally just a breeze during the daylight hours, then with the evening veering leeward, that is, turning northwest and coming from the vast plains of Patagonia and Tierra del Fuego. But the three men normally experienced a few hours of rain and with the warmer weather they had to expect storms that might change the atmospheric conditions.

Nevertheless, with the increasingly fortifying sun, vegetation was beginning to timidly emerge. The prairie beyond the enclosure had entirely lost its winter cloak, revealing a carpet of pale green. Lying under the young foliage of the Antarctic beeches would even have felt pleasant. The generously fed brook flowed, brimming, to the inlet. Moss and lichen reappeared at the feet of the trees and on the sides of the rocks, as well as that cochlearia which is so effective against scurvy. In sum in the absence of spring—for that pretty word has little currency in the Magallanes—it was summer which, for a few weeks yet, reigned on that furthermost outpost of the American continent.

At the close of the day, before the moment came to light the beacon, Vasquez, Felipe, and Moriz would sit on the little east-facing perimeter wall. Quite naturally the head keeper would initiate and keep up the conversation.

"Well, lads," he would say after conscientiously filling his pipe—imitated by the two others—"are you beginning to get used to your new life?"

"Sure, Vasquez," replied Felipe. "You can't get really fed up or tired in twenty-four hours."*

"Right," said Moriz, "but our three months'll go quicker than I'd have thought possible."

"They'll fly along my lad, like a corvette under her royal, mizzen topgallant, skyscraper, and studding sails!"

"But we've not seen a single ship today, even in the distance."

"They'll come, Felipe, they'll come," replied Vasquez, curling his hand in front of his eye as a telescope. "They wouldn't have bothered to build such a fine lighthouse on Staten Island, able to send its light ten miles out to sea, if no ships wanted to use it."

"Anyway, our lighthouse is still too new," observed Moriz.

"As you say," replied Vasquez, "and captains'll take time to find out this coast is now lit. Then they won't think twice about hugging it and running in for the strait, making their sailing that much easier! Knowing there's a lighthouse is one thing but you've got to be sure it's always on, from sunset to sunrise."

"They'll only know," Felipe thought it useful to add, "after the *Santa Fe*'s returned to Buenos Aires."

"Dead right, lad, and when Captain Lafayate's report's been published, the authorities'll soon spread the news through the whole maritime world. But most sailors must already know what's happened here."

"As for the *Santa Fe*, which only left five days ago," continued Moriz, "its journey will take . . ."

"What it takes," interrupted Vasquez. "But no longer than another week methinks. The weather's good, the sea's fine, the wind's from the right direction, the sloop has a quartering wind in her sails day and night, and, with the engine as well, I'd be surprised if she didn't make nine or ten knots."

"As we speak," said Felipe, "she must have the Strait of Magellan behind her and be at least fifteen miles past Cape Virgins."

"Certainly, my lad," declared Vasquez, "and she'll be following the Patagonian coast and can race the Patagonians' horses, even if man and beast run like the finest frigate with the wind in her yard."

It is easy to understand why the memory of the *Santa Fe* was in the good men's minds. She was part of the mother country, she had just abandoned them, and in their thoughts they would follow her to the end of her homeward voyage.

And then they discussed other things, more relevant to their practical needs on the island.

"How did the fishing go today, Vasquez?" asked Felipe.

"Not too bad. I caught a few dozen gobies and grabbed a crab—a good three-pounder that was darting between the rocks."

"That's great," replied Vasquez, "and don't worry about emptying the bay! The more you catch, the more there's left, they say, and we can keep our dried meat and bacon! As for vegetables—"

"Well," announced Moriz, "I went down to the beech copse and dug up a few good roots and I'll cook you some great grub. I saw the sloop's master cook at work—he's a past master."

"Great," declared Vasquez, "because we don't want to use the preserves if we can help it, even the best ones. They're never as tasty as stuff that's freshly killed, or caught, or picked."

"Ah!" said Felipe. "If we were to bump into a few ruminants from the interior of the island, a couple of guanacos or the like—"

"I wouldn't say no to a fine fillet or haunch," replied Vasquez. "A good piece of venison is a good piece of venison and your stomach will thank you for it. But, lads, careful not to stray too far from the perimeter while hunting big or small game. If animals show their faces, that's fine and dandy, we'll take a pot shot. But we need to stick to instructions and not stray too far from the lighthouse, except to see what's happening in Elgor Bay and out to sea between Cape San Juan and Diegos Point."

"But," replied Moriz, who enjoyed hunting, "if a nice one came within range—"

"Within range, even two or three times range, and I won't say no. But you know the guanaco's got too wild a nature for high society—ours, I mean—and I wouldn't be surprised if we only saw a pair of horns sticking above the rocks near the beech copse or the perimeter."

It was true that since the works had begun, not a single animal had been reported around Elgor Bay. The first officer of the *Santa Fe*, a determined Nimrod,* had tried several times to hunt guanacos. All his attempts had been in vain although he penetrated five or six miles inland. If larger game was certainly out there, it did not show itself within shooting distance. If he had crossed the high ground between Parry and Vancouver Points, if he had gone as far as the other end of the island, he might have had better luck. But where the high peaks stood up in the western part, the terrain was surely very difficult, and neither the first officer nor any of the crew from the *Santa Fe* ever went to explore the area around Cape Gomez.

During the night of 16 to 17 December, during Moriz's shift in the duty room, a light showed three or four miles to the east from six to ten o'clock. It was clearly a ship's light, the first in the waters round the island since the lighthouse had been built.

Moriz thought correctly that his colleagues, who had not yet gone to sleep, would be interested and went to tell them.

Vasquez and Felipe went back up with him straightaway and stood with their telescopes at the window facing east.

"It's white," stated Vasquez after observing it for a minute with the greatest concentration.

"And so," said Felipe, "it's not a position light as it's not green or red."

The remark was accurate, for position lights are placed, according to their color, to port or starboard.

"And," added Vasquez, "since this one is white, it must be on the foresail, which indicates a steamer off the island."

This seemed clear and a steamer was obviously standing in for Cape San Juan. Would it follow Le Maire Strait or pass to the south? That was the question the keepers asked themselves. So they followed the approach of the vessel and half an hour later knew what route she was following.

The steamer, leaving the lighthouse to port on the south-south-west, entered the strait. Its green light could be seen when it had Cape San Juan abeam; then it was quickly swallowed up in the darkness.

"That's the first ship to sight the Lighthouse at the End of the World!" exclaimed Felipe.

"And it won't be the last," Vasquez replied.

The following morning Felipe reported a large sailing ship on the horizon. The weather was clear, the atmosphere free of mist in a moderate southeasterly which enabled the ship to be seen at more than ten miles.

In response Vasquez and Moriz came up to the lighthouse gallery. They could make her out above the last cliffs of the shore, a little to the right of Elgor Bay, between Diegos Point and Several Point.

The ship was moving quickly, at an estimated speed of at least twelve or thirteen knots. She had a quartering wind taking her by the starboard quarter. But as she was sailing straight for Staten Island they could not say whether she would pass inside or outside.

As sea folk always interested in such questions, Vasquez, Felipe, and Moriz discussed this point and in the end Moriz proved right when he claimed the sailing ship was not heading for the entrance of the strait. When only a mile and a half from the coast she luffed so as to come more into the wind and round Several Point.

A large vessel of at least eighteen hundred tons, she was rigged as a three-master in the style of those American-built clippers of truly wonderful speed.

"May my telescope turn into an umbrella," exclaimed Vasquez, "if she doesn't hail from a New England shipyard!"

"Perhaps she'll send us her number," suggested Moriz.

"She'd only be doing her duty," replied the head keeper.

That was exactly what happened as the clipper rounded Several Point. A succession of colors and flares rose on the spanker boom, ciphers which Vasquez translated after consulting the book of signals in the duty room.

It was the *Montank** from the port of Boston, New England, in the United States of America. The keepers replied by raising the Argentine flag to the top of the lightning conductor and did not take their eyes off the ship until the tip of her mast had disappeared behind the heights of Vancouver on the south coast of the island.

"I hope," said Vasquez, "the *Montank* has a good trip and heaven spares her bad weather off Cape Horn!"

The following days the sea seemed almost deserted. At most one or two sails were glimpsed on the eastern horizon. Passing about ten miles off Staten Island, the ships were clearly not trying to stand in for the land of America. In Vasquez's opinion they were probably whalers heading for the Antarctic, the new whaling area. They also spotted a few blower dolphins coming from higher latitudes, keeping a good distance from Several Point and heading for the Pacific Ocean.

There was nothing of note until 20 December, apart from meteorological observations. The weather had become quite variable, with sudden changes in the wind from northeast to southeast. Several times fairly heavy rain fell, on occasion accompanied by hail, indicating electrical tension in the atmosphere. There was thus a danger of storms, which would surely be formidable at this time of year.

On the morning of the 21st, Felipe was smoking as he strolled on the terrace, when he thought he saw an animal near the beech copse.

After watching for a few seconds he went to get a telescope from the common room and thanks to the ten-times magnification of this instrument he could see the animal much closer to the perimeter.

This animal stood about two kilometers away, on the top of a rock formation behind the copse, and so appeared to be only two hundred meters away, perfectly visible.

Felipe realized that it was a large guanaco and perhaps the only opportunity to have a good shot at it. In an instant Vasquez and Moriz, whom he had just called, came out of the annex and joined him on the terrace. All agreed to go hunting, since if they managed to hit the guanaco, they would have fresh meat and nicely change their daily fare.

This was their decision: armed with one of the guns, Moriz would leave the enclosure and try, unseen, to work his way round the stock-still animal, to push it towards the bay where Felipe would be waiting.

"Whatever you do, be very careful, my lad," Vasquez said, "those animals have sensitive ears and noses! However far away it sees or smells you, it'll be on its guard and if it's not in range you can save your powder and shot—it'll move too fast for you to shoot or head it off. In that case, let it go because you mustn't get too far away. Understood?"

"Understood."

Vasquez and Felipe headed for the terrace and using the telescope confirmed that the guanaco had not moved since first spotted; then they focused on Moriz.

He was heading for the beech copse. He would be under cover there and could perhaps reach the rocks without frightening the animal, in order to take it from behind and force it towards the bay. His colleagues watched him until he disappeared in the wood.

About half an hour later, the guanaco had still not moved, although Moriz had to be within range.

Vasquez and Felipe waited therefore for a shot to ring out and for the animal to either fall hurt or run away as fast as it could.

However no shot came and to the great surprise of Vasquez and Felipe, the guanaco, whose head was moving back and forth as if it smelled danger, did not bolt, but instead stretched out on the rocks, its legs loose and its body crumpling as if lacking the strength to stand up any more.

Almost immediately Moriz, who had managed to slip behind the rocks, appeared and rushed towards the motionless guanaco; he leaned over it, felt it, and abruptly stood up again. Then turning towards the enclosure he gestured unmistakably to his colleagues to immediately come and join him.

"Something strange's going on," said Vasquez. "Come on, Felipe."

And the two of them, clambering down from the terrace, ran towards the beech copse.

Ten minutes was all it took to get there, and Vasquez's first question was: "Well . . . the guanaco?"

"It's here," replied Moriz, pointing to the animal lying at his feet.

"Is it dead?" asked Felipe.

"A real dodo."

"Old age then?" exclaimed Vasquez.

"No . . . a wound."

"A wound! It was hit?"

"Yes, a shot to the flank."

"A shot!" repeated Vasquez.

Nothing could be clearer. Having been hit, the guanaco had dragged itself to this spot and then dropped down dead.

"So there are hunters on the island?"*

Motionless and pensive, he cast an unquiet eye around him.

4. Kongre's Gang

If Vasquez, Felipe, and Moriz had been magically transported to the eastern end* of Staten Island, they would have seen how different the coastline was from that between Cape San Juan and Several Point. In vain would they have sought a bay of salvation for ships attacked by the Pacific storms. Here just stood cliffs rising to two hundred feet, most of them sheer but stretching far out under the deep waters, permanently lashed by aggressive breakers even in calm weather.*

Before these arid cliffs, whose clefts, crevices, and faults sheltered myriad seabirds, lay many banks of reefs, some stretching two miles out to sea at low tide. Between them wound narrow channels, passages impracticable except to small emanations. Here and there stretched beaches, carpets of sand with a few thin marine plants, strewn with shells broken by the weight of waves at high tide. Many caves lurked within these cliffs, deep, dry, dark grottoes with narrow mouths whose interiors were not swept by squalls or flooded by surf, even at the fearsome equinoxes. Access was over mounds of stones and litters of rocks, on occasion moved about by the strongest waves. As for communication with the plateau, gorges difficult to scale led up to the cliffs-tops, and reaching the arid plateau at the center of the island would have meant a detour of two or three miles.* In sum the unruliness and desolation were greater here than on the opposite coast, the one containing Elgor Bay.

Although the west of Staten Island was partly protected from the northwesterlies by the heights of Tierra del Fuego and the Magellanic archipelago, the sea broke there as furiously as around Cape San Juan and Diegos and Several Points. So, although one lighthouse had just been constructed on the Atlantic side, another was needed as badly on the Pacific one, to guide vessels that had rounded Cape Horn and were making for Le Maire Strait. The Chilean government, if it decides* to build this lighthouse one day, will perhaps be following the Argentine Republic's example.

Whatever the future held, had such works been undertaken simultaneously on the two extremities of Staten Island, they would have threatened a band of wreckers who had taken refuge near Cape Gomez.

These egregious criminals had landed at the entrance of Elgor Bay several years before. There they had lived in deep caverns* in the cliff, which offered them secure shelter, as no ship ever put in at Staten Island.

The leader of these dozen men was called Kongre, with a certain Carcante as his deputy.*

The whole bunch hailed from South America, with five of them Argentines or Chileans. The others, presumably Fuegian natives recruited by Kongre, had merely had to cross Le Maire Strait to join the gang, for they knew the south coast of the island from fishing during the fine season.

Carcante was Chilean, but nothing else was known about him, such as the town or village of the Republic he had been born in, or the family he belonged to. Thirty-five to forty years old, of medium build, rather slender but sinewy, muscular and immensely strong, a devious nature and a false heart, he would never have hesitated to commit any robbery or murder, and so was ideal to support the gang's chief.

As for the leader, nothing was known about his life. He had never mentioned his nationality. Was he even called Kongre? What seemed certain was that his name often occurred among the natives of the Magallanes and Tierra del Fuego. On the voyage of the *Astrolabe* and the *Zelée*, Captain Dumont d'Urville, putting in at Peckett Harbor on the Strait of Magellan, took aboard a Patagonian of that name.* But it was unlikely that Kongre possessed a Patagonian origin. He lacked the slightly tapered brow and broad jaw of that country's men, their narrow retreating forehead, elongated eyes, flat nose, and generally great stature, characteristics shared by all the tribes. Moreover, his physiognomy did not present the gentle expression found in most of the inhabitants of Patagonia.

Kongre's temperament was violent and energetic, as evident from his fierce features, ill-concealed by a thick beard already turning white, although he was only about forty. A true bandit, a dangerous evildoer, stained with every crime, the only hiding place he had been able to find was this deserted island, whose interior had never been explored.

How Kongre and his companions had been able to live on the island for the years since they sought shelter on it will now be briefly explained.

When Kongre and his accomplice Carcante fled Punta Arenas,* the main port of the Strait of Magellan, following a series of crimes punishable by the noose or garrote, they managed to reach Tierra del Fuego, where it was difficult to pursue them. While living among the Pécherais, they learned of the great frequency of wrecks on Staten Island, not yet lit by the Lighthouse at the End of the World. Its shores were covered with all sorts of wreckage, some of it valuable. Kongre had the idea of organizing a gang of wreckers, with two or three similar scoundrels the pair had fallen in with in Tierra del Fuego, plus about ten Pécherais, just as worthless. A native boat took them across Le Maire Strait. But although Kongre and Carcante were both mariners, having sailed for years on the dangerous waters of the Pacific, disaster struck. A very rough sea threw them on the rocks of Parry Point, where their vessel broke up.

It was then that they reached Elgor Bay, known to some of the Pécherais. Their hopes were not dashed. Every beach between Cape San Juan and Several Point was covered with wreckage, old or new: bales still intact, chests of provisions that would feed the band for many months, easily repairable firearms including revolvers and rifles, ammunition well-protected in metal cases, bars of gold and silver of immense value from rich Australian cargoes, furniture, planks, boards, wood of all sorts, here and there a few skeletons, but not a single survivor from all these maritime disasters.

This formidable Staten Island was in fact well known to navigators, and the construction of a lighthouse on its eastern end had been essential for a number of years. Without seeing it, one could not possibly have an idea of the accumulation of reefs at the approaches to Elgor Bay, stretching a mile or two out to sea. Every storm-tossed ship driven onto its coast was inevitably lost with all hands.

The gang did not settle at the end of the bay, but at its mouth, more suited to Kongre's plans, as he could watch Cape San Juan. Quite by chance he discovered a spacious cavern, with a mouth concealed by thick marine vegetation, seaweed, and sea wracks. It was spacious enough for the band to live in and safe from the sea winds, sheltered as it was behind a cliff buttress on the north side of the bay. Into it they carried everything from the wrecks that could serve as furniture, bedding, or clothing, with a large number of tins of meat, boxes of biscuit, and kegs of brandy and wine. They used a second cave near the first to store all the wreckage of value, including the gold, silver, and jewelry found on the beaches. If Kongre later managed to treacherously lure a ship into the bay and seize it, he planned to load all the plunder onto her and return to the Pacific islands that had witnessed his earliest acts of piracy.

Up to now this opportunity had not arisen, and the wrongdoers had been unable to leave Staten Island. Over two years, it is true, their wealth had steadily increased. New wrecks had occurred from which they had derived great profit. Indeed, they themselves produced the catastrophes, following the example of wreckers on the dangerous shores of the Old and New Worlds.* When the easterly hurricanes raged at night, if a ship came within view of the island, they lured her in by lighting fires in the line of sight of the reefs, and if by rare chance one of the shipwrecked sailors managed to drag himself out of the waves, they butchered him on the spot. Such was the criminal work of these criminals whose very existence was unknown—for no communication existed with Tierra del Fuego or the Magellanic archipelago—and who added to the list of wrecks in these waters of the Atlantic.

However, the band remained prisoners on the island. Kongre had been able to wreck a few ships, but not to lure them into Elgor Bay, where he would have tried to seize them. Moreover, no ship had come of her own accord to anchor at the end of the bay, little known to skippers. Any crew would of course have needed to be strong enough to resist the fifteen or so bandits.

As time passed the cave began to overflow with the valuable loot from the wrecks. The impatience and rage of Kongre and his men is easy to imagine. Carcante and his chief talked about nothing else.

"To be stuck on this island like a ship on the coast," he exclaimed over and over again, "when we've got a cargo worth several thousand piasters!"*

"Okay," would come Kongre's answer; "we've got to get away, whatever happens."

"When and how?" Carcante would retort. But to such questions no answer ever came.

"Our food will run out eventually," Carcante would add. "If we can always fish, soon there may be no animals left. And think about the cold weather on this island then! When I consider the damn winters where we'll have to just grin and bear it!"

What could Kongre reply? He was a silent, uncommunicative sort of person. But what anger boiled inside him as he felt his helplessness!

No, he couldn't do anything—anything at all! Failing a ship which the pirates could surprise at anchor, if a Fuegian canoe had ventured near Parry Point, Kongre could easily have seized it. And then, if not he himself, at any rate Carcante and one of the Chileans could have embarked. Once on the Strait of Magellan, some opportunity would have arisen to get to Buenos Aires or Valparaiso. With the money, of which they had plenty, they could have bought a vessel of 150 or 200 tons, which would have sufficed.* With a few sailors, Carcante could have brought it back to Elgor Bay via the Magellanic archipelago, only a fortnight's navigation. And once the ship was safely in the inlet, the crew could easily have been got rid of. Then the whole band would have embarked with their wealth to head for the Solomons or the New Hebrides!*

Matters were at this stage when, fifteen months* prior to the opening of this story, the situation suddenly changed.

At the beginning of October 1858, a steamer flying the Argentine flag appeared off the island and maneuvered into Elgor Bay.

Kongre and his comrades at once recognized it as a man-of-war, which they dared not attack. After hiding any sign of their presence and blocking the openings of both caves, they withdrew inland to wait for the ship to go away.

She was the *Santa Fe*, bringing from Buenos Aires the engineer commissioned to construct a lighthouse on Staten Island, who had come to select the site. The sloop remained in Elgor Bay for only a few days, and then left without discovering the lair of Kongre and his men. However, Carcante had crept down to the inlet one night and had been able to find out why the *Santa Fe* had put in at Staten Island.

A lighthouse was to be built on Elgor Bay!

The gang had no choice, it seemed, but to leave their island stronghold, and that is certainly what they would have done had they been able.

Kongre did the only thing possible. The sloop would soon return with the team of men to begin work. Kongre already knew the western part of the island around Cape Gomez, where there were other caves he could hide in. Not wasting a day, since the sloop would soon be coming back with men to begin work, he carefully moved everything required for a year's stay, having good reason to believe that nobody would visit this coast while the work went on. But he did not have time to clear both caves. He had to be satisfied with removing the provisions,* the tinned food, drink, bedding, and clothing, as well as some of the precious objects; and then, carefully closing up the mouths of the caves with stones and dry grass, there was every chance they would not be discovered.

One morning, five days after the evil band had gone, the *Santa Fe* reappeared at the entrance to Elgor Bay and occupied her former mooring in the inlet. Workmen and materials were offloaded. The site on the terrace was chosen; building work began straightaway and, as described above, pushed ahead.

Thus it came about that Kongre's band were forced to take refuge at Cape Gomez. They drew all the water they needed from a stream fed by melting snow. Fishing and a certain amount of hunting allowed them to economize the provisions they had brought from Elgor Bay.

But it was with fierce impatience that Kongre, Carcante, and their companions waited for the lighthouse to be finished and the *Santa Fe* to leave, knowing she would not bring the relief team back for another three months.

Naturally Kongre and Carcante, while being careful not to be seen, ascertained all that went on at the end of the bay. By skirting the south or north littoral, approaching from inland, or observing from the nearby heights or Parry or Vancouver Points,* they could easily monitor the progress of the work and deduce when it would be finished. It was then that Kongre planned to carry out an idea he had long meditated. Now that Elgor Bay was going to be lit, who could say whether some ship might not put in there, some ship that he could seize after surprising and massacring the crew?

Even if the sloop's officers decided to make an excursion to the western part of the island, Kongre had little reason to worry. Nobody would be tempted, this year, to explore the surroundings of Cape Gomez, over the bare plateaus and impracticable ravines, all those mountainous parts to cross at the price of enormous exertions. The captain would perhaps decide to circumnavigate the island, it was true. But he would probably not try to land on this coast littered with reefs and in any case the band would take care not to be discovered.

In fact, this eventuality did not occur, and the month of December arrived, when the lighthouse was due to be completed. The lighthouse keepers would be left alone—as Kongre knew only too well—as soon as the lighthouse cast its first beams over the waters of the Atlantic.

During these last weeks, accordingly, one or other of the gang always came to keep watch on one of the peaks from where the lighthouse could be seen at a distance of seven or eight miles, with orders to return the moment the light came on for the first time.

It was Carcante himself who brought the news back to Cape Gomez, on the night of 9 December.

"Yes," he exclaimed, joining Kongre in the cave, "the devil lit it in the end, and may the devil put it out again!"

"We don't need his help!" the chief answered, his angry fist gesturing in the appropriate direction.

A few days went by, and at the beginning of the following week Carcante, while hunting near Parry Point, wounded a guanaco with a shot. As we saw, the animal escaped and fell on the very spot where Moriz saw it, outside the fringe of rocks near the clump of beeches. From that day on Vasquez and the other two keepers, knowing they were no longer the only inhabitants of the island, kept closer watch on the area around Elgor Bay.

The day came for Kongre to leave Cape Gomez and return to Cape San Juan. The pirates had decided to leave their stores in the cave. They would merely take enough for one day, relying upon those of 22 December.* By leaving at daybreak and taking a route they knew across the mountainous inland region of the island, they could do half the journey on the first day's march. After this stage of about fifteen miles, they would halt for the night, maybe under trees or rocks. Traveling along the coast would have increased the distance, given the irregular coast cut with inlets and flanked with headlands, and their tiredness would have doubled, together with the time taken. Moreover they would have run the risk of being seen from the top of the lighthouse after passing Parry or Vancouver Point—a danger avoided on the inland route.*

After the night halt, Kongre planned to begin even before sunrise the next day and start a second stage to Elgor Bay of about the same length, which he might be able to complete that evening.

Kongre guessed only two keepers were attached to the lighthouse, whereas there were in fact three. But it did not matter, all things considered. The gang was stronger than Vasquez, Moriz, and Felipe, who would not suspect a presence outside the perimeter. The pirates would surprise them in a night attack. First they would overcome two of them in the quarters, and then easily get rid of the third in the duty room.*

Thus Kongre would be master of the lighthouse. After that he would have plenty of time to fetch all the stores from Cape Gomez and if necessary put them back in the cave at the entrance to Elgor Bay.

Such was the plan mapped out in the mind of this dangerous criminal. It appeared only too certain to succeed. But whether fortune would favor him afterwards did not seem so clean.

Matters would no longer be under his control. It was essential that some vessel anchor in Elgor Bay. That anchorage would be well known to navigators after the *Santa Fe* had got back home. Also, the new beacon would light the eastern coast of Staten Island. Caught in bad weather, or unable to haul off when pushed by sea winds, a ship, especially of medium tonnage, would not hesitate to take refuge in a bay henceforth indicated by a light, rather than flee on an unleashed sea, either through the strait or south of the island . . . And then, this ship might fall into these criminals' hands and give them the long-awaited chance to escape to the Pacific, and so avoid punishment for their crimes.

But everything needed to go smoothly before the sloop returned to relieve the keepers. If they had not left the island by then, Kongre and his men would have to head back to Cape Gomez.

And in such a case things would no longer be the same. When Captain Lafayate discovered that the three lighthouse keepers had disappeared, it would seem clear that they had been abducted or murdered, and search parties would scour the whole island. The sloop would not leave again until it had been explored from Cape San Juan to Cape Gomez. How could the gang avoid capture, and how could they manage to live, if the situation lasted for long? If necessary, the Argentine Government would send other ships. Even if Kongre succeeded in getting hold of a Pécherais boat—very unlikely—the strait would be watched so carefully that he could no longer cross it and hide out in Tierra del Fuego. Would fortune favor these pirates, then, to the extent of allowing them to leave the island while there was still time?

On the evening of the 31st,* Kongre and Carcante were strolling on the tip of Cape Gomez, talking and, as sailors do, studying the sky and sea.

The weather was not good. Clouds were gathering on the horizon. A breeze blew from the northeast and would not have favored a ship wishing to enter Le Maire Strait from the west.

It was half past six. Kongre and his companion were about to return to their usual hideout when Carcante said:

"Is it agreed we leave all our stuff at Cape Gomez?"

"Yes, Carcante. It'll be easy to fetch later, when we control the whole island, and . . ."

Kongre did not finish his sentence. Focusing on the open sea, he stopped:

"Look! Look there—off the point!"

Carcante scanned the sea in the direction indicated.

"Hey!" he said. "Definitely—it's a ship!"

"Coming up to the island, by the looks of it, and on the short tack, for she has the wind ahead."

A ship under full sail was indeed tacking about, a couple of miles from Cape Gomez.

Despite the contrary wind, the vessel gradually made way, and would reach the strait before nightfall.

"It's a schooner," said Carcante.

"Of a hundred and fifty or two hundred tons."

The vessel clearly wanted to get to the strait rather than double Cape Gomez. The only question was whether she would succeed before night fell.* With the wind dropping, might the current not carry her onto the reefs?

The whole band of pirates gathered at the end of the cape.

It was not the first time, since they had been there, that they had seen ships come so close to Staten Island. As has been mentioned, these looters tried to lure them onto the rocks using moving lights.

Somebody suggested the same employing stratagem.

"No," said Kongre, "this schooner mustn't founder! We want to grab her. The wind is against her; it's going to be a dark night. She won't be able to get into the strait. We'll find her still off the cape tomorrow morning, and then see what to do."

An hour later the vessel disappeared into the pitch black night, without any light betraying her presence out at sea.

During the night the wind changed and veered southwest. At dawn, when Kongre and his men went down to the beach, they discovered the schooner stranded on the reefs of Cape Gomez.

5. The Schooner *Maule*

Kongre was no amateur in the sailing business, for he had been a ship's captain. But only his fellow mariner Carcante, who had been his second-in-command, and still was on Staten Island, could have said what ship Kongre had commanded and on what seas. However, he chose to say nothing.

It would surely have been no insult to this pair of scoundrels to throw the epithet of pirate in their faces. They must have followed that criminal profession in the waters off the Solomon Islands and New Hebrides, where ships were frequently attacked at that time. And there could be no doubt that after evading a fleet organized in that part of the Pacific by the United Kingdom, France, and the United States, they had taken refuge first in the Magellanic archipelago, and then on Staten Island, where they had switched from pirating to looting wrecked ships.

Five or six of Kongre and Carcante's companions had also been sailors, as fishermen or in the merchant marine, and were consequently familiar with the ways of the sea. As for the Fuegians, they would round out the crew if the gang managed to seize the schooner.

The schooner, judging from her hull and masts, was not designed to carry more than 150 to 160 tons. During the night, a westerly squall had run her onto a rocky sandbank, on which she could easily have broken up, although her hull seemed intact. Listing to port, her prow turned obliquely landward, her starboard flank faced the open sea. In that position her deck was visible from the forecastle to the aft deckhouse. The masts were intact—the mizzenmast, mainmast, and bowsprit with their tackle—and the sails were half-gathered, except that the mizzen, foreroyal, and topmast sails had been taken in.

The previous evening, when the schooner had been sighted off Cape Gomez, she had been fighting a fairly strong northeaster. Sailing close to the wind, she took a starboard tack and attempted to enter Le Maire Strait. This was the situation where Kongre and his companions had lost sight of her in the darkness. Then, during the night, the wind had suddenly veered, as it often does in these waters, becoming a sou'wester. Presumably the schooner had found herself too close to shore, and the bracing of her yards showed that she had been unsuccessfully attempting to move away—when she ended up square on the sandbank.

Regarding the captain and crew, one could only conjecture. But seeing themselves carried by the wind and current onto a dangerous coast bristling with reefs, they had almost certainly launched the longboat. They felt positive their ship was going to break up on the rocks, and knew the danger of perishing down to the last man. An unfortunate idea, for the boat soon capsized, and in fact, had the captain and his men remained on board they would have survived safe and sound. There now seemed no doubt they had perished, for not a single man could be seen, and their bodies had surely been swept away by the descending tide.

Boarding the schooner at ebb tide was not difficult. Starting from Cape Gomez, one could go from rock to rock to where the ship had stranded, not more than half a mile away. Kongre and Carcante did exactly that, with two of the men. The others stayed at the foot of the cliff to watch for survivors from the wreck.

When Kongre and his companions reached the sandbank, the schooner lay high and dry. But since the tide would rise seven or eight feet, the ship would clearly regain her draft if her bottom was unscathed.

Kongre had been right when he estimated the schooner's burden at 160 tons. He worked his way round the ship and read from the board at the stern: *Maule*, Valparaiso.*

So it was a Chilean ship that had been wrecked on Staten Island in the night of 27 to 28 December.

"Just the job!" said Carcante.

"If she hasn't got a hole in her hull," added one of the men.

"We can fix a hole or any other damage," was Kongre's simple reply.

Next he went to examine the flank facing the sea. It did not appear damaged. The bow, slightly embedded in the sand, also seemed intact, as did the stern post, and the rudder still held to its fittings. No firm conclusions could be drawn about the part of the hull resting on the sandbank, since it was impossible to inspect the exterior, but after two more hours of rising tide Kongre would know.

"All aboard!" he said.

Although the ship was listing at an angle that made it easy to embark at the port side, they could not walk on deck. They had to drag themselves over it by crawling along the ship's rail, so Kongre and his men held on to the mainmast shroud as they did so.

The impact could not have been very severe for, apart from a few loose spars, everything seemed in position. The schooner, not having a very trim design, was not leaning at a severe angle, and she would surely right herself with the tide, if, that is, she had no damage to her vitals to let in water.

Kongre's first care was to slide as far as the deckhouse, whose door he opened with some difficulty. At the left of a very small wardroom he found the captain's cabin. He went in, bracing himself against the walls, took the ship's papers from a drawer in a cupboard, and came back to the aft deck where Carcante waited.

Together they examined the ship's articles, and this is what they found:

"Schooner *Maule*, Port of Valparaiso, Chile, burden 157 tons. Captain Pailha* and crew of six left in ballast, 3 December. Destination Falkland Islands."

These islands, also known as the Malvinas, are located about three hundred miles from Tierra del Fuego.* The *Maule*, after successfully rounding Cape Horn, had been preparing to enter Le Maire Strait when she foundered on these reefs of Staten Island. Neither Captain Pailha nor his men had lived to tell the tale, for a survivor would have sought refuge at Cape Gomez, and nobody had appeared in the two hours since daybreak.

The schooner was not carrying cargo, since she was heading in ballast for the Falklands. The essential thing for Kongre was to have a ship at his disposal to get away from the island, along with his loot. And he had one if he managed to refloat the *Maule*.

The ballast, consisting of a higgledy-piggledy pile of old iron, would have had to be moved in order to check the inside of the hull. To do so would be time-consuming, and the schooner would be vulnerable if the sea wind freshened. It was better to tow her off the sandbank as soon as she began floating on the tide. The sea would soon start to rise, and it would be high water in a few hours.

So this is what Kongre told Carcante:

"We'll get everything ready to tow the schooner as soon as she's got enough water under her keel. She may not have serious damage and may not take on water."

"We'll know soon enough, for the tide's turning. What are we going to do then?"

"We'll shift the *Maule* off the reefs, through the narrows beside Cape Gomez, and then steer her to the end of the inlet in front of the caves. She won't touch bottom there even at low tide, since her draft's only six feet."

"And then?" asked Carcante.

"And then we'll load everything that came from Elgor Bay."

"And . . . ?"

Kongre merely replied, "We'll see."

They set to work, for if they missed the next tide, the refloating of the schooner would be delayed another twelve hours. They absolutely needed to anchor her in the inlet before midday. There she would always have enough water, and would be relatively secure if the weather held.

First of all Kongre, helped by his men, removed the anchor from the starboard bow and moved it some distance from the sandbank, using the whole length of the chain. In this way, as soon as the keel was off the sand, it would be possible to tow the schooner into deeper water. They would have enough time to reach the inlet before the tide went out, and so carry out a full inspection of the hull in the afternoon.

These measures were taken quickly, and completed by the time the tide came in. The sandbank was about to disappear under water. Accordingly, Kongre, Carcante, and half a dozen companions climbed on board, while the others headed back to the foot of the cliff.

All they could do now was wait. Often a sea wind freshens with the rising tide—their great worry, for it might strand the *Maule* more or push her further onto the bank, which was higher to landward. The tide was now almost high, and it appeared possible the sea might not rise sufficiently to free the schooner if she were pushed half a cable towards the coast.*

But everything seemed to favor Kongre's plans. The wind rose a little, veering southwest, which would help the *Maule*. Kongre and the others stood at the bow, which would normally float sooner than the stern. If, as they hoped, the schooner were to pivot on her bottom, they would just need to use the capstan to turn her prow seawards and then, towed on her chain, about fifty fathoms long, she would be back in her element.

45

Meanwhile the sea slowly rose. A few shivers indicated the hull was feeling the action of the tide. The waves were coming in in long swells, and even out to sea there were no breakers. No one could have wished for more favorable conditions.

Yet even if Kongre now felt certain he could free the schooner and take her to safety in the inlet of Cape Gomez, one eventuality still worried him. Might the hull of the *Maule* not have been stove in on the port side, the side resting on the sandbank, which they had not been able to inspect? If some leak were present there, they would not have time to move the ballast and patch the hole. The schooner would not lift from the bed, she would fill up, and they would have to abandon her here, to be destroyed by the first storm.

This was a major worry. How impatiently Kongre and his companions watched the rising tide! If some of the planking was disjointed or the caulking had worked loose, the water would soon invade the hull and the *Maule* would not even be able to right herself.

But little by little they became calmer. The sea was gaining. Each second the hull appeared deeper in the water. The tide was rising up her sides and not flowing in. A few tremblings indicated that the hull was intact, and the deck gradually righted itself again.

"No leaks, no leaks!" exclaimed Carcante.

"Man the capstan!" ordered Kongre.

The cranks stood ready. Four men were merely waiting for the order.

Leaning over the bow rails, Kongre watched the tide, already rising for an hour and a half. The foredeck was beginning to wobble and the front section of the keel no longer touched; but the stern post was still sunk in the sand, and the helm did not enjoy free play. No doubt another half hour would be required for the stern to be freed.

Kongre decided then to speed up the refloating, and while remaining at the bow he cried:

"Haul away!"

The vigorously turned cranks were able merely to tighten the chain, and the stem did not turn seaward. Since there was a danger of the anchor dragging, making it difficult to fix again, Kongre abandoned the attempt.

By now the schooner had completely righted herself. Inspecting the hull, Carcante was able to check that no water had come in. In other words, if there was damage, at least the planking was still in position. It could even be hoped that the *Maule* had not suffered any harm, either when running aground or during the dozen hours spent on the sandbank. In that case its anchorage in the Cape Gomez inlet would be short. They would load her up in the afternoon and she would be ready to go to sea again the very next day. In any case they needed to employ the weather. The wind would help the *Maule*, whether she followed Le Maire Strait or the southern coast of Staten Island as far as the Atlantic.

At about nine o'clock the tide would be in, and, as they always say, a quarter tide is never very high. But in the end, given the schooner's relatively small draft, it was conceivable she would leave the sandbank.

Indeed, shortly after half-past eight, the stern rose slightly. The *Maule* pivoted without risking damage, because the swell was arriving gently and she had run aground on a sandy stretch.

After examining the situation once more, Kongre considered towing might be attempted with some chance of success. His men began to turn the cranks, and after drawing in a dozen fathoms of the chain, the stem of the *Maule* turned seaward. The anchor had taken the strain. Its flukes were stuck solidly in a crack in the rocks, and would have broken before being pulled out by the capstan.

"Heave ho!"

And everybody set to, even Carcante, while Kongre leaned over the taffrail and watched the stern of the schooner.

There were a few moments of doubt. The other half of the keel was still scraping the sand.

Kongre and the others felt worried. In twenty minutes the sea would no longer be rising, and the *Maule* needed to be refloated by then, or else lie stranded till the next tide. The tide was due to diminish for two days and would only resume its strength forty-eight hours later.

The moment had come to make a last effort. One can imagine the fury, more than the fury, the rage of these men when they found themselves helpless! To be standing on the ship they had so long lusted after, which would give them freedom, and probably impunity as well, and be unable to wrest her from this sandbank!

So oaths and curses exploded as they hauled on the capstan, always afraid the anchor might break or slide. They would have to wait for the evening tide to drop this anchor again or add a second one. But who knew what might happen in twenty-four hours, or whether atmospheric conditions would still be as favorable?

Indeed, a few thickish clouds were beginning to rise in the northeast. True, if they stayed in that direction, the ship's situation would not worsen, since the sandbank lay in the lee of the high cliffs along the coast. But might the sea not roughen, and the swell finish off what the grounding had begun the night before?

But also the northeast winds, even as breezes, would be unfavorable to navigation in the strait. Instead of making for the open sea, the *Maule* would be forced to keep very close to the wind for several days, and in matters of navigation delays can often have serious consequences.

The sea was now slack, and in a few minutes would begin to change. The whole of the sandbank was covered. Only a few tips of reefs could be seen at sea level. The point was no longer visible from Cape Gomez. And the last sandbar on shore, after being caressed briefly by a wave, remained high and dry. Clearly the sea would soon begin to withdraw, and the rocks around the bank would soon emerge.

Curses arose anew, and the men, exhausted and panting, were about to abandon a task which could no longer succeed.

Kongre ran up to them, fury in his eyes, anger overflowing. He picked up an axe and threatened the first man to desert his post. It was clear he would not hesitate to use it.

All set to work again, and with the crank's efforts the chain grew taut enough to break, stripping the copper sheathing off the mooring holes.

Finally a noise was heard. The capstan idle had just moved a notch. The schooner had made a slight movement towards the sea, wiggling, and the wheel indicated she was little by little freeing herself from the sand.

"Hooray! Hooray!" shouted the men as they sensed the *Maule* coming free. Her bottom had just slid over the sand. The capstan accelerated, and a minute later the schooner, having completely hauled in her anchor, was floating off the bank.

Immediately Kongre rushed to the wheel. The anchor, aweigh, was stowed on the bow. They only needed now to sail into the narrows between the reefs to reach the Cape Gomez inlet.

Kongre set the jib, which would surely suffice. Given the condition of the sea, there was enough water everywhere. Half an hour later the schooner rounded the last rocks on shore and anchored just behind the cape.

6. At Elgor Bay

The refloating operation, then, had been a complete success.* But it did not follow that the schooner was now entirely safe in her cove at Cape Gomez. True, the rocks acted as cover to the south and east, thanks to the curvature of the point, and the shore cliffs protected her from easterlies. But in every other direction she was exposed to squalls, to the assaults of storms, and even to swells from the open sea.* In the season of strong equinoctial tides, she would not have lasted twenty-four hours.

Kongre was well aware of it. His intention was to leave the cove at ebb tide the following day, for he wanted to use the tide to navigate part of Le Maire Strait.

But first he had to finish inspecting the ship and check the condition of the hull from the inside. It was certain that she had not taken in water. But even though her planking had not been damaged when she ran aground, her rib might have been, in which case repairs would be needed before she could make a voyage of any distance.

So Kongre put his men to work. They displaced the ballast filling the hold as far as the port and starboard floor planks. They would not need to unload it, which saved time and effort—time in particular, which they must not waste in the perilous situation the *Maule* now found herself in.

First the scrap metal ballast was moved to the aft end of the hold so they could check the forward sheathing. Kongre and Carcante did the inspection with the help of a Chilean named Vargas,* a former shipyard carpenter from Valparaiso who knew the business well.

No damage was visible from the stem to the mizzenmast step. Floor timbers, rib, and planking were in good condition; their copper pegs had not suffered from running aground on the sandbank.

With the ballast moved forward, things also appeared intact from the mizzenmast to the mainmast. The pillars supporting the deck had not warped or buckled, and the ladder to the central hatch was in place.

Then they examined the third and last area of the hold, from the bottom of the counter to the stern post. Here the damage was considerable. There were no leaks, but the port rib showed a depression a meter and a half long, obviously the result of a collision with a rock before running aground on the sandbank. The planking had not moved very much, and the caulking remained in place, so that no water had entered the hold. But the damage seemed serious enough to give a sailor good reason to worry. Repairs would be required before heading out to sea, except for a very short voyage, and even then only on condition the ship encountered calm weather and did not labor too much. In sum the repair would probably require an entire week, even if Vargas had the materials and tools needed.

Kongre and his companions knew what they were up against. The cheers that had greeted the refloating of the *Maule* now gave way to curses, appropriate in the circumstances. Would the schooner turn out to be useless? Would they be unable to leave Staten Island after all?

Kongre interrupted:

"The damage is really serious. We can't count on the *Maule*, as she might come apart in bad weather. We've got hundreds of miles to do before we reach the islands of the Pacific. We'd risk sinking on the way. But this damage can be repaired, and we'll do it."

"Where?" asked one of the Chileans, not hiding his anxiety.

"Not here, anyway," declared one of his companions.

"No," replied Kongre in a resolute tone. "In Elgor Bay."

All things considered, that seemed feasible. The schooner could cover the distance in forty-eight hours. She just needed to follow the island's coastline, either south or north. In the cave containing the loot from the wrecks, the carpenter had the wood and tools needed for the repair. The *Maule* could even lie there for two or three weeks if necessary. The fine weather was due to last two months. And when Kongre and his men did leave Staten Island, it would be on a perfectly safe ship, with her damage repaired.

In fact, Kongre had always intended to spend some time at Elgor Bay after leaving Cape Gomez. Whatever happened, he was not willing to lose the diverse items he had left in the cave when the lighthouse work had forced the band to flee across the island. The only change in his plan was that his stay would now be longer. In any case he had no choice.

So confidence returned, and they prepared to sail at high tide the following day.

The presence of the lighthouse keepers did not worry Kongre and his companions. What could the keepers do against these thugs?

As soon as they were alone, Carcante said a few words on this subject to Kongre. He received the following reply:

"Before this schooner arrived I'd decided to take over Elgor Bay anyway. When we arrive it won't be difficult to get rid of the keepers. Instead of crossing the island unseen, we'll arrive openly by sea. The schooner will appear and anchor in the inlet. They'll welcome us, without suspecting anything, and then—"

He concluded with a gesture Carcante could easily understand, and indeed the plan had every chance of success. Short of a miracle, how could Vasquez, Moriz, and Felipe escape their fate?

The gang spent the afternoon preparing for departure. Kongre had the ballast put back in place and busied himself loading the provisions, weapons, and other items brought to Cape Gomez.

Everything was quickly loaded. Since leaving Elgor Bay more than a year before, Kongre and his companions had eaten most of their reserves of food, and what remained was now placed in the ship's storeroom. For the bedding, clothing, cutlery, kitchen items, gold, and silver, there was plenty of room in the galley, the crew's quarters, the aft deckhouse, and the hold. They had not yet loaded any of the material still in the cave at the mouth of Elgor Bay.

They worked so diligently that the cargo was on board by four in the afternoon, and the schooner could have left. But Kongre did not want to sail at night along a shore covered with shoals reaching several miles out to sea, nor was he at all sure whether to follow Le Maire Strait to Cape San Juan. That would depend on the wind direction, and not whether it stayed northerly and began to freshen.* In the latter case he preferred to sail south of the island so the *Maule* would be sheltered by the land. In any case he estimated that the voyage would last no more than thirty hours, including the layover at night.

By evening the weather had not changed. There was no mist in the sunset, and the line of sky and water was so clear that a green ray* crossed the sky at the very instant the disk was disappearing below the horizon.

It seemed the night would be calm, and indeed it was. Most of the men spent it on board, some in the crew room, others in the hold. Kongre occupied the cabin of Captain Pailha, on the right of the wardroom, and Carcante that of the first officer, on the left.

Several times they came on deck to study the sky and sea, checking that even high tide would not put the *Maule* in danger and that nothing would delay their departure the next day.

The sunrise was superb, on a clear horizon rarely seen at that latitude. At first light, Kongre landed in the longboat and, following a narrow ravine near the beginning of Cape Gomez, reached the cliff top.

At this point his eyes ranged over a vast area of water, three-quarters of the compass. Only to the east did it encounter the distant masses between Parry and Vancouver Points.

The sea appeared calm to south and west. It was a little rough at the opening of the strait, since the wind was beginning to freshen. But neither sail nor steam were visible, and the *Maule* would certainly not encounter any ship on her short voyage to Cape San Juan.

Kongre made the decision on the spot. He had good reason to fear that the wind would pick up, and he did not want to make the schooner labor by exposing her to swells from the strait, which are always a problem when the tide turns. He decided to follow the southern coast, arriving at Elgor Bay via Several and Diegos Points. The distance was more or less the same by either route, north or south.

Kongre came back down to the shore, headed for the cavern, and made certain that nothing had been left to betray the presence of a troop of men on the western tip of Staten Island.

It was a little after seven o'clock, and the tide was already beginning to ebb. That would make it easier for the ship to navigate the narrows that culminated outside the shoals.

The anchor was immediately brought in, and the foresail and jib hoisted. With a northeaster, this would be enough to take the *Maule* past the banks, so she quickly set sail. Kongre stood at the helm, while Carcante watched the bow. In ten minutes they were free of the shoals, whereupon the schooner began pitching and rolling slightly.

On Kongre's order, Carcante set the mizzen and spanker, which is a schooner's mainsail. Then he raised the topsail chock up. With sails hoisted and trimmed, the *Maule* stood in for the southwest, with the wind on the quarter, so as to round the far tip of the island.

In half an hour the *Maule* had passed the rocks of Cape Gomez. She then headed east,* half a mile from land, a point alee so as to haul as much wind as possible. Sheltered as she was by the southern coast of the island, the wind helped her along.

Meanwhile Kongre and Carcante had been able to observe that this slender vessel sailed well at all points. She would risk nothing by venturing into the Pacific in fine weather, after leaving behind the last islands of the Magellanic archipelago.

Kongre might have managed to reach the entrance to Elgor Bay by evening, but then the schooner would have passed Several Point rather late, and he preferred to enter the bay before the sun disappeared. So he did not crowd the sail, and used neither the mizzen topgallant nor the mainmast topsail, but kept to an average of five or six knots.

On her first day out, the *Maule* encountered no other ships. Night was about to fall when she put in on the other side of Vancouver Point, having completed about half her voyage.

Here rose enormous piles of boulders and the highest cliffs on the island. The schooner anchored a cable length from shore, in a cove sheltered by the point. No vessel could have had a more tranquil harbor or dock.

Of course, if the wind had veered south, the *Maule* would have been very exposed. The coast of Staten Island is directly assaulted by polar storms, and the sea is as violent as around Cape Horn.

But it seemed as if the wind would remain northeasterly. Luck was certainly favoring the plans of Kongre and his men!

The night of 2 to 3 January* was extremely calm. The wind had abated at about ten in the evening, but increased again towards four, at the approach of day.

At first light Kongre was making preparations. The sails, now drawn in on their brails, were set, the capstan hauled the anchor into its station, and the *Maule* was under way.

Vancouver Point stretched about five or six miles into the sea, extending due south, so the schooner had to make her way to a coast that ran eastward as far as Several Point, a distance of about twenty miles.

As soon as the *Maule* had reached the shore with its peaceful waters sheltered by high cliffs, she was sailing in the same conditions as the day before.

What a dreadful coast, more terrible even than the strait! Unstable piles of boulders encumbering the shore except at high tide! A vast expanse of blackish shoals where not even the smallest ship or even boat could put in! Not one inlet for landing, not one sandbank for setting foot! What a monstrous rampart Staten Island had thrown up against the terrible Antarctic swells!

The *Maule* moved along under moderate sail, less than two miles from the coast. Kongre did not know this area, and had good reason not to come too close in. But he stayed in calmer waters than would have been encountered further out to sea. He did not wish to make the *Maule* labor more than she had to.

As things turned out, the second day's sailing had been rapid enough to bring the *Maule* to the latitude of Several Point by about three o'clock. After rounding the point, to be at the mouth of Elgor Bay she just had to head north for six or seven miles.

It seemed likely that by sunset she would be back at her old anchorage, below the lighthouse in the little inlet where the *Santa Fe* had set sail twenty-three days ago.

Kongre, however, was well aware that beyond this point the *Maule* would be slowed down by several hours' struggle against increasing northeasters. If they happened to freshen at the moment the tide turned, it would be difficult for the *Maule* to maintain her position while the current was taking her from below. In that case, perhaps Kongre would even have to take shelter behind Several Point and wait one more day before heading for the bay.

But since he was impatient to complete his voyage that very evening, he made ready to round Several Point.

He needed first of all to move further out to sea, since the point stretched east a good two miles. Even now, although the wind was not strong, he could see the waves frothing and the sea breaking violently on the point, for at this tip of the island the waters are agitated by a great confluence of the Atlantic and Pacific currents. Here the sea is in constant turmoil, and the waves collide with a roar even when calm prevails around the rest of the island.

The wind was blowing northeasterly, and it would be against them until they entered the bay. The schooner would need room to turn alee, without lying into the wind more than forty-five degrees. There would be several hours of very difficult and tiring navigation.

This entire stretch of the eastern coast was a wretched place, defended as it was by a barrier of fearsome shoals. Kongre would be wise to keep a certain distance out.

He came to take the wheel, and at his command Carcante tightened the sheets so as to sail as close to the wind as they could. If the shape of the coast were to shift the wind northward, as often happens, the *Maule* might progress without having to tack. In that case she might make Diegos Point at the mouth of the bay without laboring too much, which was to be avoided as much as possible.

Finally the schooner, having sailed a good three miles out to sea, turned north, tacking to starboard. At this distance the whole coast was visible, from Cape San Juan to Several Point.

At that moment the Lighthouse at the End of the World came into view, and Kongre saw it for the first time. Taking the telescope from Captain Pailha's cabin, he could make out one of the keepers, scanning the sea from his post on the gallery. The sun was due to remain above the horizon for another three hours.

The keepers had surely spotted the schooner, and recorded her arrival in the waters of Staten Island. As long as Vasquez and his colleagues saw it heading due northeast, they would think she was heading for the Falklands. But now that she was sailing into the wind, wouldn't they wonder whether she was trying to enter the bay?

But little did Kongre care whether the keepers had spotted the *Maule* or even thought she was going to drop anchor. That would not change his plans in any way.

To his huge satisfaction, it looked as if the second half of his voyage would be accomplished in good conditions. The wind had shifted a little to the north. With her sheets hauled flat aft, ready to shake in the wind, the schooner started up again towards Diegos Point, with no need for tacking.

This was a very fortunate situation. Considering the condition of her hull, she might not have been able to withstand repeated tacking, which would have made her labor. And for all anyone knew she might spring a leak before she could arrive at the inlet.

That is exactly what happened. When the *Maule* was two miles from the bay, one of the men climbing down a rope into the hold came back on deck shouting that water was coming in through a crack in the planking.

This was the exact place where the *Maule* had collided with a rock. The planking had held, but now gaped open, if only for a distance of a few inches.

In sum the damage was not very serious. Vargas moved the ballast and managed to stop the hole using a wad of cotton stuffing, and the water almost stopped coming in. But one can imagine how essential a careful repair was going to be. Because of the stranding on Cape Gomez, the schooner would have been lost if she had ventured into the Pacific.

It was six o'clock when the *Maule* found herself at the mouth of Elgor Bay, a mile and a half from shore. No longer needing the topgallant sails, Kongre had them furled. Only the topsail, main jib, and spanker remained hoisted. With the wind abreast, and sails set in this manner, the *Maule* would have no difficulty reaching her mooring on the inlet of Elgor Bay.*

In addition—and this must not be forgotten—Kongre perfectly knew the route he was following, and would be able to act as pilot.

In any case, at about half past six a beam of bright rays shone over the sea. The lighthouse had just been lit. And the very first ship whose path across the bay it illuminated was a Chilean schooner, fallen into the hands of pirates* who were returning to the scene of their crimes and preparing to commit others.

It was nearly seven, with the sun setting behind the high peaks of Staten Island, when the *Maule* passed Cape San Juan to starboard. The bay lay open before them as far as Diegos Point, and she entered it under light sail. An hour would suffice to reach the foot of the lighthouse.*

As they passed the cave, dusk left enough light for Kongre and Carcante to check* that its entrance had not been discovered behind the pile of rocks and curtain of underbrush. Nothing had given away their presence on this part of the island, and they would be able to recover their loot.

"It's working like clockwork," said Carcante to Kongre, with him at the stern.

"Soon it'll be going even better."

No more than forty-five minutes* later, the *Maule* arrived at the inlet where she was to anchor. She was hailed by two men who had just come down to shore from the terrace.

Felipe and Moriz were preparing their launch to board the schooner. Vasquez had remained on lookout at his post. Accordingly Kongre and his men assumed that only two men were responsible for looking after the lighthouse.*

When the schooner had arrived in the middle of the inlet, her spanker and topsail were taken in, together with her main jib, whose sheet Carcante had brought down. Darkness was beginning to fall at the end of Elgor Bay when they dropped anchor.

Moriz and Felipe jumped on deck.

Suddenly, at a sign from Kongre, the former received an axe-blow to the head and fell fatally wounded. At the same time two revolver shots hit Felipe, who fell next to his colleague. A final cry* and the pair breathed no more.

Vasquez heard the shots through a window in the lookout post, and saw the crew of the schooner murdering his colleagues.

He would suffer the same fate if he fell into their hands. He could expect no mercy from such killers. Poor Felipe! Poor Moriz! He could do nothing to save them. He stayed where he was, horrified by the frightful crime that had taken place in a few seconds! After the first moment of stupor, when he had recovered his ability to think, his self-control returned and he considered the situation. He must escape the attacks of these thugs at all costs. Once they had finished the task of anchoring,* some of them might get the idea of going up the lighthouse. And—who knows?—their aim might be to put it out, and make the bay impracticable, at least until day broke.

Vasquez did not hesitate. He left the duty room and rushed down the stairs. On reaching the living quarters he found no one, for the good reason that no one had yet disembarked.*

He had not a moment to lose, for he could hear the launch leaving the schooner. Some of the crewmen were about to land.

Vasquez took two revolvers and slid them into his belt, then stuffed some supplies into a bag and threw it over his shoulder. Unnoticed, he rushed out of the quarters and down the lighthouse perimeter, and was lost in the darkness.

7. The Cavern

What a horrible night the unfortunate Vasquez would be spending! What a plight! His poor colleagues murdered and thrown overboard, the tide even now carrying their bodies out to sea! Had he not been on duty at the lighthouse, he would have shared their fate. Yet he thought only of them, not of himself.

"Poor Moriz! Poor Felipe!" he repeated, and large tears fell from his eyes. "They went to offer help to those wretches, suspecting nothing! And in return they got pistol shots! I'll never see them again . . . and they'll never see their country or their families either! And Moriz's wife! To wait another two months for him, and then find out he's dead!"

Vasquez was sobbing. They were dear to him, the two keepers under his charge, for he had known them for many years. It was he who suggested they ask to work at the lighthouse. And now he was alone. Alone!

But where had the schooner come from? What pirate crew did she have on board? Had they seized her and murdered her captain and crew? What flag did she sail under? And why were they anchoring in Elgor Bay? Did they know the bay, then? On that subject there could in fact be no doubt, for no captain would have placed his ship in such danger otherwise. So what were they doing here? And why did they stop the lighthouse working as soon as they went ashore? Was it to prevent ships taking refuge in the bay?

These questions crowded into Vasquez's mind, but he had no answers. He was not even thinking of his own danger. But soon these criminals would notice that the quarters were occupied by three keepers. So where was the third? Wouldn't they set out to look, and wouldn't they end up finding him?

It must be reiterated that Vasquez was not thinking of his own safety. From his hiding place on the bay shore, less than two hundred paces from the inlet, he could see lights moving, sometimes on board the schooner, sometimes within the lighthouse perimeter or through the windows of the quarters. He could even hear the men talking loudly to each other in his own tongue. So were they compatriots of his? Or Chileans? Peruvians? Bolivians? Mexicans? Brazilians? They all speak Spanish!*

Finally, at about ten o'clock, the lights went out. No further sound troubled the dark night.

But Vasquez could not stay here. At daybreak they would find him. He had no hope of pity from these bandits. He had to escape their reach.

What direction should he choose? Further inland, where he would be a bit safer? Or the mouth of the bay, and hope that if some vessel came in sight he could signal her and have some chance of rescue? But whether he went inland or stayed on the coast, how to stay alive until relief came? His food would soon be used up. In less than forty-eight hours he would have none left, and how could he get more? He did not have so much as a fishing rod! And how could he make a fire? Would he be reduced to mollusks and shellfish?

In this moment he hardly considered the future. He thought only of his two poor colleagues, and wept.

But in the end his energy prevailed. He needed to take a decision, and so he took one. He would head for the coast of Cape San Juan and spend the night there. Tomorrow he would consider the situation.

So Vasquez left the place where he had stood observing the schooner. No sound or light was coming from her. The criminals knew they were safe in this inlet, and had probably left no one on guard on board.

Vasquez followed the left bank, working his way along the foot of the cliffs. He heard nothing but the plash of the outgoing tide and the occasional cry of a bird tardily returning to her nest.

It was eleven when he stopped at the corner of the bay. On the shore below the cliff, the only shelter he found was a narrow crevice. He remained there until daybreak.

Before the sun had lit the horizon, Vasquez went down to the shore to see if anybody was coming, whether from the lighthouse or around the cliff at the end of Cape San Juan.

This part of the coast was entirely deserted, on both banks of the bay. Not a boat to be seen, although now the crew of the schooner had two available, the longboat of the *Maule* and the keepers' launch.

No ship was visible off the island.

And Vasquez began to think how dangerous it would be to sail the waters of Le Maire Strait, now that there was no functioning lighthouse. Ships arriving from the open sea would no longer know their position. Expecting to encounter a light at the end of Elgor Bay, they would head west, running the risk of being cast on that awful coast between Cape San Juan and Several Point.

"They cut the light! The criminals!" exclaimed Vasquez. "And since it's not in their interests to light it again, they won't!"

Switching off the lighthouse had indeed created a grave situation. Even without moving, these evildoers could benefit more from the resulting disasters. They no longer needed fires to attract ships, which would come trustingly to take a bearing on the lighthouse.

Vasquez sat on a slab of rock and thought about all that had happened yesterday. He gazed at the bay, imagining he might catch sight of his poor colleagues' bodies as the current carried them away. No, the tide had already done its work and the deep had swallowed them up.

At that moment the situation appeared to him in all its terrifying reality. What could he do? Not a thing. Nothing except wait for the return of the *Santa Fe*. But it would be two long months before the sloop appeared again at the mouth of Elgor Bay. Even if the crew of the schooner did not capture him, how could he feed himself?

He would always be able to find shelter in some grotto in the cliff, and in any case the warm season was due to continue at least until the relief came. If it had all happened in the middle of winter, Vasquez could never have stood the cold. The thermometer falls to thirty or forty degrees below zero, and he would have frozen to death if not already dead from starvation.

First of all, Vasquez looked for shelter. He was sure the criminals would visit the living quarters and realize that the lighthouse had been managed by a team of three. They would want to get rid of the third by any means, and soon they would pay a visit to the area around Cape San Juan.

It should be said again that all Vasquez's energy had returned. Despair had no hold on his strongly tempered character. Through his deep faith this old sailor trusted God not to abandon him and never to allow these bandits to avoid punishment for their crimes.*

After a few searches Vasquez found a cranny, a small burrow of ten by five or six feet, near the corner of the cliffs on the shore of Cape San Juan. With a floor of fine sand, it was beyond the reach of high tide and sheltered from the full blast of the sea winds. Slipping into the hole, Vasquez set down the supplies from his sack and the items he had taken from the living quarters. A rio fed by melted snow ran along the foot of the cliffs toward the bay, meaning he would not go thirsty.

Feeling some hunger pangs now, he assuaged them with some biscuit and corned beef. He was about to go out and fetch some water when a sound nearby made him freeze.

It's them! He said to himself.

Stretching out near the wall, so as to see without being seen, he looked towards the bay.

A boat with four men was following the current. Two manned the oars at the bow. The other two sat at the stern, one of them holding the tiller. It was the longboat, not the lighthouse launch.

What are they doing here? Vasquez wondered. Are they looking for me? From the way the schooner sailed into the bay, these criminals know it well, and this isn't their first trip to the island. They didn't come just to visit the coast. If it's not me they're after, what's their game?

Vasquez observed the men and concluded that the oldest of the four, the one at the tiller, must be the leader and schooner's captain. He could not say what his nationality might be. But his men, from their appearance, seemed to be South Americans of Spanish descent.

The boat was now almost at the entrance to the bay. It was following the left bank, a hundred paces from the hole where Vasquez hid, watching closely.

The leader, on a sign from the rowing stopped. One sharp turn of the tiller, and the boat's momentum beached it gently on the shore.

The four men quickly got out. One of them threw the grapnel and dug it in the sand.

Then these words reached Vasquez's ears:

"So it's here, is it?"

"Yes. The cave's over there, twenty paces from the corner of the cliff."

"Dead lucky those lighthouse fellows didn't find it!"

"Not even the ones who spent fifteen months building it!"

"Right! They were too busy, over at the end of the bay."

"But also the entrance was so well hidden!"

"Let's go!" said the leader.

The beach was about a hundred paces wide at this point. The leader and two of his companions made their way diagonally to the foot of the cliff.

From his position Vasquez followed every movement, turning his ear to catch every word. The sand strewn with seashells crunched under their feet, but this soon stopped, and Vasquez saw nothing but the man pacing up and down beside the boat.

They've got some sort of cave there, he said to himself, but what's inside?

Vasquez was now certain that the schooner had brought a gang of sea-roving plunderers, and that they had been living on Staten Island before the work had begun. So was it this cave they had hidden their loot in? And were they planning to load it onto the schooner?

Suddenly a thought occurred to him. Surely they had stocks of provisions, which he could put to good use?

Something like a ray of hope slid into his soul. As soon as the boat had gone back to the schooner, he would leave his hole, locate the cave entrance, go inside, and find enough to live on until the sloop arrived! The wish of this man of resolution, if his life was spared for a few weeks, was for these criminals to be unable to leave the island.

"Yes! If only they're still here when the *Santa Fe* comes back, then Captain Lafayate will make them pay for their crimes!"

But would his wish come true? Having reflected, Vasquez told himself that the schooner was surely going to anchor in Elgor Bay for two or three days. That'd be plenty of time to load the cargo from the cave. Then she'd leave Staten Island, never to return. In any case, he would soon know the truth.

After an hour in the cave, the three men reappeared and walked along the shore. From his hiding place in the hole, Vasquez could still hear them talking loudly, sharing information that would be useful to him.

"Eh, those great guys left plenty for us when they were here!"

"And the *Maule* will have plenty when she sails!"

"Piles of grub for the trip, which gets us out of a mess!"

"Especially as what's on board now wouldn't get us to the Pacific islands!"

"And for a whole year, they never found our treasure, or came to bother us at Cape Gomez!"

"We'd have really wasted our time, wrecking those ships here, if we didn't get lots out of it!"

Vasquez heard these criminals as they joked among themselves, and his heart raged. He was temped to rush in front of them, revolver in hand, and crack all three of their skulls. But he controlled himself. Better not to lose any of this conversation. He had learned what an abominable profession the men followed on this part of the island, and he was not surprised when they added:

"As for their precious 'Lighthouse at the End of the World,' I'd like to see captains try and find it now! They're sailing blind!"

"They'll keep blindly going for the island, and their ship will be smithereens!"

"I just hope one or two get wrecked on the rocks of Cape San Juan before the *Maule* leaves! I want our schooner loaded to the gunnels, since the devil sent her to us!"

"And the devil doesn't mess around! We got a fine vessel at Cape Gomez without a single crewman! No captain, no sailors! We'd have got rid of them anyway!"

So that explained how a schooner called the *Maule* had fallen into the gang's hands. They had lived on the left bank of Elgor Bay for several years until the lighthouse work had made them flee to the west of the island. That was why so many ships had been lost with all hands and cargo, lured in by these pillagers' tricks.

"And now Kongre," asked one of the three, "what are we going to do?"

"Go back to the *Maule*, Carcante," said this Kongre, whom Vasquez had correctly imagined the leader of the gang.

"When are we going to start clearing out the cave?"

"Not until the ship's repaired. And that's obviously going to take a good week or more."

"In that case, let's take a few tools with us."

"Yes . . . We can come back when we need more. Everything Vargas needs for his work is here."

"Let's get on with it, Kongre," added Carcante. "The tide will be coming in again, and help us."

"Okay. When the schooner's ready, we'll load up the cargo. No danger of the cave being robbed."

"Hey . . . Kongre, don't forget there were three lighthouse keepers, and one got away."

"I'm not worried about that one. He'll be dead in three days unless he lives on moss and seashells. In any case we'll block off the cave entrance."

"All the same," said Carcante, "it's a shame we have to do any repairs. The *Maule* could have set off tomorrow. Admittedly, while we're still here some ship may come and hit the coast without us even needing to lure her in. And what she's got won't be wasted!"

Kongre and his companions came out of the cave again, carrying tools and pieces of planking. Then, having taken care to close up the entrance, they went back down to the boat and embarked just as the tide started coming in.

The boat shoved off straightway. With the oars pushing it along, it soon disappeared behind a promontory.

Once there was no danger of being spotted, Vasquez went back to the shore. He now knew all he needed to about two important questions. First, he had several weeks' supply of food. Second, the schooner had sustained damage which would require at least a fortnight to repair, perhaps even longer, although surely not enough to keep her until the sloop arrived.

How could Vasquez have thought of delaying the schooner's departure once she was seaworthy? Yes, if some ship did happen to pass close to Cape San Juan, he'd make signals. He'd throw himself into the sea and swim to her if he had to. Once on board, he'd tell the captain everything. If the captain had a large enough crew, he wouldn't hesitate to make for Elgor Bay to seize the schooner. If the criminals fled to the interior, they'd never be able to leave again. And when the *Santa Fe* returned, Commander Lafayate would know exactly where to capture the gang or destroy them down to the last man! But would such a ship come into view off Cape San Juan? And unless she passed within a few cable lengths, would she even notice his signals?

As far as he himself was concerned, he would be able to avoid their searches. Kongre knew of the existence of a third keeper but was not worried about him. But the important thing was to find out whether he would have enough food until the sloop arrived. And so Vasquez headed for the cave.

8. Repairing the *Maule*

To repair the damaged schooner, ready her for a long voyage across the Pacific, load her with the cargo from the cave, and set sail as soon as possible: this was the job Kongre and his men had taken on, and they intended to waste no time.*

All in all, repairing the *Maule*'s hull would not amount to a huge job. Carpenter Vargas knew what he was doing. He had all the tools and materials needed, and he had the right conditions to get the job done.*

But first they needed to remove the ballast, and haul the schooner into the inlet. Then they would have to bring her about to repair her exterior and replace some of the planking in her hull.

So it might take some time, but Kongre had plenty. The fine weather was due to last two long months more.

He knew about the arrival of the relief ship, for the ledger in the keepers' living quarters had told him everything he needed to know. Relief was due only every three months. The sloop *Santa Fe* would not be coming back to Elgor Bay until early March, and it was now only the beginning of January.

The ledger also identified three keepers, Moriz, Felipe, and Vasquez, and the bedroom was laid out for three. So one of them had managed to avoid his colleague's fate. Where he had hidden seemed of little consequence; as we know, Kongre did not care much whether this man even remained on the island. Alone and without resources, he would soon succumb to want and hunger.

Yes, they had plenty of time to repair the schooner, although they would have to allow for possible delays. And in fact, no sooner had they set to work than they found themselves unable to continue.

The problem was an abrupt change of weather on the night of 3 January. Indeed, if the *Maule* had traveled to Elgor Bay twenty-four hours later, she would probably have been destroyed on the rocks of Several Point.

That night saw massive clouds crowding the southern horizon. The temperature rose to sixteen degrees while the barometer fell to storm level. Lightning flashed continually, and thunder rolled in from all directions. Furious gales were unleashed, the sea raged in across the reefs, and breakers whitened the cliffs' peaks. Any vessel, under sail or steam, would have been in grave danger of dashing herself against the island's coasts, however great her tonnage—to say nothing of a ship of as small a burden as the *Maule*.

So fierce was the tempest that at high tide a swell from the open sea swept through the bay, rose against the cliffs, and engulfed the shore. Waves broke against the quarters, with the spray flying as far as the beech copse, half a mile inland.

Kongre and his companions devoted their energy to keeping the *Maule* at anchor. Several times she tugged on it, threatening to wreck herself on the coast, and they had to cast a second anchor to reinforce the first. On two occasions the men had reason to fear total disaster.

Even as they watched over the *Maule* day and night, the gang were moving their berths to the annexes and away from the terrors of the storm. Once they had brought the bedding in from the cabins and crew's quarters, there was plenty of room for the approximately fifteen men. Never in their entire stay on Staten Island had they known such luxury.

Nor had they cause to worry about food or drink. Had there been twice as many mouths to feed, the lighthouse provisions would have lasted more than three months.* The reserves in the cave would also be available if necessary. In short, the schooner had enough supplies for a long voyage on the Pacific.

As work was impossible, an entire week went to waste. Kongre thought it unwise to remove the ballast, for the schooner was pitching and rolling like a rowing boat and the men were already busy ensuring she did not hit the rocky bottom. She would have wrecked herself there just as surely as on her arrival at Elgor Bay.

The wind changed that night and veered abruptly south-southwesterly. The sea became very rough in the direction of Cape Gomez, with a stiff breeze. If the *Maule* had remained in her cove at the cape she would surely have been reduced to matchsticks.

One ship passed Staten Island that week. Since it was daylight, she paid no attention to the lighthouse, and could not have noticed that it was no longer lit between sunrise and sunset.* She was following a northeaster into Le Maire Strait, a French flag at her gaff.

They needed a telescope to see her nationality, for she passed two miles from shore. This meant that if Vasquez signaled her from Cape Tucuman, she could not have seen the signals—and did not see them, for a French captain would not have hesitated to send the longboat to take him aboard.

On the morning of the 13th, the scrap metal ballast was unloaded onto the sand, safe from the tide. The hull could now be inspected more thoroughly than at Cape Gomez, and the carpenter considered the *Maule* more seriously damaged than at first supposed. She had labored greatly after rounding Several Point, sailing close to the northeaster, struggling in a rough sea, and springing a leak in the aft part of her hull. In fact, she would not have been able to go any further than Elgor Bay. More than four feet of her frame and planking needed to be replaced, and the most efficient way to do that was on dry land.

Thanks to the items stored in the cave, which as we know were of all sorts and functions, carpenter Vargas had no shortage of materials. He was confident of completing his work with the help of his comrades. The *Maule* would never be able to venture into the Pacific waters unless she was properly repaired. It seemed especially fortunate that the masts, sails, and rigging had not been damaged. Of course, the name *Maule* and that of her home port would need to be altered before she began her voyage.

The first task was to ground the schooner on the sand so that she would list to starboard. Having no heavy machinery, they would have to make use of the tides. There was a wait of a couple of days until the sea would be sufficiently high to carry the schooner onto the beach and leave her high and dry when it went out again. Such a tide would come with the new moon, not due for four more days.*

Kongre and Carcante used the wait to revisit the cave, this time in the lighthouse launch, larger than the *Maule*'s boat. In it they could bring back the valuable objects: gold, silver, and jewelry from their looting, and other precious items to be stored in the annex.

The launch left on the morning of 14 January. The tide had been ebbing for two hours and was due to turn in the afternoon.

The weather was quite fine. A breeze pushed the clouds northward, the sun's rays shining between them.

Before leaving, Carcante went up to the gallery to scan the horizon, his daily practice. The open sea was empty, with not a single vessel in the strait. Not even a Pécherais fishing smack, such as appeared occasionally near Parry Point. As far as the eye could see, the island appeared just as deserted.

As they followed the current, Kongre studied the left bank. About half a mile from the lighthouse, it was about five or six hundred fathoms from the opposite shore. So where was that third lighthouse keeper who had escaped the massacre? He seemed hardly worth bothering about, but it would have been better to get rid of him, although it could be done in due course.

The bank was as deserted as the bay. Only the myriad birds nesting in the cliffs provided signs of life, crying and flying about.

At about eleven, the launch landed near the cave. With the sail and jib set, the launch had been helped along by the wind as well as the tide.

Kongre and Carcante disembarked, leaving two men on guard, made for the cave, and emerged half an hour later.

They had quickly observed that everything seemed as they had left it, although it would have been difficult even by lamplight to find anything missing in such a profusion of stuff.

Kongre and his companion brought out two sealed cases from the wreck of a British three-master, containing a considerable sum in gold specie and precious stones. When they had put the cases in the launch, and were about to set off, Kongre announced that he had decided to head for Cape San Juan, in order to scan the shore to the south and north.

So he and Carcante made for the right bank and walked to the tip of the cape. From there the eye could range as far as Several Point in one direction and in the other a long two miles of the shore doubling back along Le Maire Strait.

"Not a soul," said Carcante.

"No."

The tide was turning as they reboarded the launch and sailed back down the current. By three o'clock they had reached the end of Elgor Bay.

Two days later, on the morning of the 16th, Kongre and his companions proceeded with the grounding of the *Maule*. The tide would rise at about eleven, so they planned carefully. When the water was high enough, a mooring line along the ground would allow them to haul the schooner onto the shore. The task itself presented no difficulty, as the tide would do nearly all the work.

As soon as the sea had risen enough for the schooner to move forward over the beach, they hauled on the hawser, having no more than ten fathoms to clear.

They now needed only to wait for the tide. At about one o'clock, the water began to reveal the rocks near the cliffs; at two, the keel of the *Maule* touched the sand; and at three, she lay high and dry on her starboard flank.

Now they could begin work. As they had not been able to take the schooner up the beach to the foot of the cliff, she would be afloat for a few hours each day at high tide, meaning the work would have to halt. But since each tide after 16 January would be a little lower than the one before, the down time would gradually reduce and the work could then continue for a fortnight uninterrupted.

The carpenter set to work. If he could not count on the Pécherais members of the gang, at least the others, including Kongre and Carcante, would assist him.

It was now possible to work on both the interior and exterior of the schooner. The damaged sheathing proved easy to take off after removing the copper sheets from the ship's bottom. That exposed the timbers and frames which needed replacing. The planks and sheathing from the cave would be adequate, so there was no need to chop down and saw up a tree from the beech copse, a major operation.

Over the next fortnight, assisted by fine weather, Vargas and the others worked well. What caused the most difficulty was removing the frames and timbers that needed replacing, as they had been pegged with copper and bound with trenails. The whole held together well, showing that the schooner came from one of the finest shipyards in Valparaiso. Only with difficulty did Vargas finish the first part of his task, which he certainly could not have done without the carpentry tools from the cave.

Naturally, the tide interrupted their work for the first few days. But after that it barely reached the first slopes of the beach, so the keel no longer came in contact with the water and they could work on the hull interior as well as the exterior. It was important that the planking be in place before the tide began to return.

In any case, there was no need to make the schooner list to port when the repair had been done on that side. The starboard hull had not hit, and after careful examination Vargas was able to conclude that running aground on Cape Gomez had caused no harm on that side at all. Much time would be saved.

But as an extra precaution, and without going so far as to remove the copper bottom, Kongre wanted to make certain that all the seams above the water line were resealed with tar and cotton packing salvaged from shore.

Thus they pursued their task, working almost without interruption until the end of January. The fine weather continued, in the sense that there were only a few hours, rather than days, of rain, although sometimes very heavy. Yet it remains true that weather problems are always a worry in such a variable clime.

During this period two vessels were sighted in the waters off Staten Island. The first was a British steamer coming from the Pacific. Following Le Maire Strait before heading northeast, she was probably making for a European port. She emerged from Le Maire Strait in full daylight, at least two miles from Cape San Juan. Having appeared after sunrise and disappeared before sunset, her captain could not notice the absence of the lighthouse.

It proved impossible to determine the nationality of the second ship. Night was falling when they sighted her off the tip of Cape Gomez, about to follow the island's southern coast to Several Point.* Carcante, on duty in the lookout room, saw only the red light on her port side. But if this sailing ship had been at sea for several months, perhaps her captain and crew were unaware that the lighthouse had already been completed.

This second vessel sailed sufficiently close to the coast for its men to have noticed any signal, such as a fire at Vancouver or Several Point. Did Vasquez attempt to attract their attention? Whatever the truth, by sunrise the vessel had disappeared to the east.

They also spotted other ships under sail or steam on the horizon, probably heading for the Falklands, which would probably not even have sighted Staten Island.

The first days of February saw very high tides and a radical change in the weather. The wind veered southwest, and directly assaulted the mouth of Elgor Bay.

Although the repairs were not entirely finished, it seemed most fortunate* that at least the timbers, frames, and sheathing had been replaced and the *Maule* was now assured of a watertight hull. No more fear of leaks in the hold.

Congratulations were in order. For forty-eight hours, at high tide, the sea rose up the hull, almost to the water line, and the schooner even righted herself, but without her keel being freed from the sand.

Kongre and his companions were going to have to take every precaution against any new damage, which might delay their departure considerably.

Most fortunately, the schooner continued to be held firmly by her grounding. She rolled from side to side with some violence, but ran no risk of being thrown onto the rocks of the inlet.

But from 4 February the tide was lower, and the *Maule* rested more firmly on the shore. Caulking the hull was now feasible, and there was a sound of mallets from dawn to dusk.

Loading the cargo would not delay the *Maule*'s departure. On Kongre's orders, the men not assisting Vargas took the launch on frequent visits to the cave, sometimes accompanied by Kongre and sometimes by Carcante.

Each time they brought back more cargo for placing in the hull of the schooner, which would need no more than a third of her ballast. For the present everything was put in the lighthouse store room. This was much more convenient and simple than if the *Maule* had loaded in front of the cave at the mouth of the bay. There the weather might have interfered, since there was no shelter on this coast, leading to Cape San Juan.

In a few more days the repairs would be completely finished, the *Maule* seaworthy, and the cargo ready for loading.

On the 13th, they finished caulking the *Maule*'s deck and hull, and even managed to repaint her, stem to stern, using a few pots of paint salvaged from the carcasses of the wrecks. Nor did Kongre neglect to make a few essential repairs to sails or to trim the rigging, which must in any case have been new when she sailed from Valparaiso.

In short, the *Maule* would have been ready to return to the inlet for loading as early as 13 February. But despite the impatience of Kongre and his companions, however eager they were to leave Staten Island, they needed to wait another forty-eight hours for a tide high enough to refloat the schooner and bring her to anchorage in the middle of the inlet.

Such a tide occurred on the morning of 15 February. The keel rose from her berth in the sand; and now all they needed to think about was the cargo.

In a few days, barring accidents, the *Maule* would venture forth from Elgor Bay and down Le Maire Strait, head southwest, and scud at full sail for the seas of the Pacific.

9. Vasquez

A fortnight had passed since the schooner had dropped anchor in Elgor Bay, and during that time Vasquez had remained on the coast of Cape San Juan. He felt most reluctant to leave. If some ship came and anchored in the bay, he would at least be able to hail her. Once aboard, he would warn the captain of the danger were he to sail up to a lighthouse held by a gang of bandits. If his crew were insufficient to fight the bandits and either capture them or put them to flight inland, at least he would have time to head for the open sea.

But how likely did such an eventuality seem? Why would a vessel try to anchor at the entrance to a bay hardly known to sailors, unless she were forced to?

It was in any case the best chance. The ship could then have done the few days' voyage to the Falklands, where the British authorities would be notified of events on Staten Island, and might send a warship to Elgor Bay. The ship would arrive before the *Maule* could get away, and destroy Kongre and his gang to the last man. Then the Argentine government would act quickly to restore the operation of the lighthouse.

"So should I wait for the *Santa Fe* to return?" Vasquez kept asking himself. "But she's not due back for another two months. By then the schooner will be miles away. How could anyone find her among the islands of the Pacific?"

As we know, the good Vasquez still thought about his colleagues, murdered without pity. He thought of the criminals, how they might avoid punishment by leaving the island. And he considered how dangerous these waters would be for ships, now that the Lighthouse at the End of the World no longer sent out its beams.

But in terms of resources, his situation seemed reassuring—provided his hideout was not discovered. After he had visited the cave, he had no fear that he would lack food once Kongre left.

This huge cavern went a long way back into the cliff. The gang had hidden there for several years, with enough room for Kongre and his companions. They had piled it with all sorts of salvage from the many wrecks on Staten Island, plus gold, silver, and precious objects gathered from the shore at low tide. The cavern had been where they lived. Although they must have quickly used up whatever they had on disembarking at Parry Point, the first shipwreck, as we saw, had provided enough to live on. The gang had caused new disasters, and profited from them.

Then the construction of the lighthouse began. Kongre had been obliged to leave the bay, taking with him everything his gang needed to live at Cape Gomez. They therefore left most of their loot in this cavern, which unfortunately had not been discovered while the work was proceeding.

Vasquez planned to take only what he needed, so that Kongre and his men would not notice anything missing. And among so many different sorts of objects, who would notice a few missing kitchen items, tins, or munitions?

On his first visit he accordingly satisfied himself with a few things: a small box of sea biscuit, a cask of corned beef, a cooking stove, a kettle, a cup, a woolen blanket, a spare shirt and stockings, an oilskin, two revolvers with about twenty cartridges, a lighter, a lantern, and some tinder (for he had enough flotsam on the coast). He also took two pounds of tobacco for his pipe. He had overheard that it would probably take two or three weeks* to repair the schooner and so he would always be able to come and get more.

In point of fact he considered his little grotto rather too near the cavern. To prevent discovery he found another shelter, somewhat further away and more secure.

At a distance of five hundred paces, on the coast beyond Cape San Juan where the shore was low, opened a grotto. Its only entrance was indistinguishable from a pile of rocks between two large boulders standing against the cliff. To reach it, one had to slip through a crack, almost invisible among the rocks. The sea approached at high tide, but never far enough to enter the grotto, and its fine sand contained no seashells or dampness. One could have passed the cave a hundred times without noticing it, and Vasquez had only found it by pure chance a few days earlier. Here he moved everything he had taken from the gang's cavern.

Kongre, Carcante, or any of the others visited this part of the coast only rarely. Since their second trip to the cavern, Vasquez had spotted them only once, when they had stopped at the tip of Cape San Juan. Crouching at the bottom of the space between the boulders, he couldn't be seen, and wasn't.

Obviously he never ventured out of his hiding-place without taking every possible precaution, preferably in the evening, especially when heading for the gang's cavern. Before turning the corner of the cliff at the bay's mouth, he always made certain that neither the longboat nor the lighthouse launch was tied up on shore.

How endless the time seemed in his solitude! And how often he remembered that tragic scene he had fled! Felipe and Moriz falling under the assassins' attacks! An irresistible desire arose in his heart. He longed to meet the leader of the gang. He dreamed of avenging with his own hands the death of his ill-fated comrades.

"Yes, yes!" he said to himself. "Some day they'll be punished. God won't let them escape. They'll pay for their crimes with their lives."

And he forgot that his own life hung by a thread as long as the schooner still anchored in Elgor Bay.

"Those criminals mustn't leave!" he repeated. "Not until the *Santa Fe* comes back! May Heaven stop them sailing away!"

Would that come to pass? It was still only late January, more than three weeks before the sloop was due to appear off the island.

Vasquez still felt puzzled that the schooner remained so long at her mooring. What could the reason be? Was she so badly damaged that the repairs would take a month? Having read the lighthouse ledger, Kongre must know that the relief team were due at the beginning of March. And if he had not put to sea by then . . .

It was now 16 February. Vasquez, devoured with impatience and worry, wanted to know what he was up against. After sunset he made for the entrance to the bay, working his way up the left bank towards the lighthouse.

Even in utter darkness, he might be noticed if one of the gang were to come his way. He slid along the cliff, scrutinizing each shadow, stopping and listening to every suspicious sound. The air was calm, and he took care to step quietly.

Vasquez had three miles to cover to reach the end of the bay. He was retracing the path of his flight after the murder of his comrades, and he remained as unseen as that evening.

It was about nine o'clock when he stopped two hundred paces from the lighthouse perimeter, and saw some lights in the annex window. An angry, threatening gesture escaped him as he thought of the bandits occupying these quarters in place of those they had murdered—and the man they would still murder, if he fell into their hands!

From his position Vasquez could not see the schooner, hidden in the shadows. Considering it safe to do so, he came a hundred paces closer. The whole gang were behind closed doors, and it was unlikely anyone would come out of the quarters.

Vasquez moved still closer, as far as the shore of the little inlet. At high tide the previous day the schooner had been hauled from the sandbank. Now she was afloat and anchored!

Ah, if only it were in his power to stave in her hull and sink her in this inlet! But it was impossible.

Clearly the damage had been repaired. They needed merely to load the cargo, taking two or three days, and then she would sail out of the bay and onto the high seas!

There was nothing Vasquez could do but retrace his path to Cape San Juan and the grotto where he had spent so many sleepless nights.

The schooner was afloat. Yet he had noted that she lay not on her water line, but two feet above it. This indicated that she had no significant ballast or cargo on board, and that her departure might be delayed a few days. That, however, would be the last reprieve. In perhaps forty-eight hours the *Maule* would round Cape San Juan, cross Le Maire Strait, and disappear westwards towards the distant Pacific shores.

Vasquez now had only a small amount of food left. Accordingly the following day he headed back to the cavern to get more.

Day was only just breaking. Nonetheless, he told himself that the launch would be coming back this morning to take everything for loading on the schooner. He moved carefully but swiftly.

Rounding the cliff, he saw no launch, just a deserted shore, so ventured into the cavern.

Much was still there, although none of it was of any special value, presumably meaning Kongre did not want to fill up the *Maule*'s hull with it. But when Vasquez looked for the biscuits and meat, his hopes were dashed.

All the provisions had disappeared! In forty-eight hours he would have nothing to eat!

Vasquez had no time to think, for at that moment he heard the sound of oars. It was the launch, with Carcante and a pair of his cronies.

Vasquez rushed to the entrance of the cavern, stuck out his head, and looked.

The launch was already landing. He barely had time to dash back inside and into the darkest corner. Here he hid behind a pile of sails and spars, left behind as there was no room for them on the schooner.

Vasquez resolved to sell his life dearly if the bandits found him. He always carried his revolver at his belt, and he would certainly use it. But one man against three!

Only two entered the cave, Carcante and carpenter Vargas. Kongre's head was the one Vasquez wanted to split open, but he had not come along.

Carcante held a lighted lantern. Followed by Vargas, he picked out the final items to load onto the *Maule*. They chatted as they searched:

"It's already 17 February. We'd better get a move on," said the carpenter.

"Yes, we'll get a move on."

"Tomorrow?"

"Tomorrow, I imagine. We're ready in any case."

"If the weather behaves itself."

"Yes, and it looks a bit nasty this morning. But it'll get better."

"Because if we're still here in eight or ten days—"

"Don't even think about it," exclaimed Vargas. "We could never take on a warship!"

"No, they'd take *us*," Carcante shot back. "Probably on both ends of their mizzen yard!"

He followed this observation with an impressive curse.

"All I know is that right now I'd rather be a hundred miles out to sea."

"Tomorrow, I said tomorrow!" Carcante replied firmly. "Unless we get the kind of wind that knocks the horns off guanacos!"

Vasquez listened to this exchange without moving, almost without breathing. Carcante and Vargas went back and forth carrying their lanterns, shifting things around, putting aside the ones they were going to take. At times one of them came so close to his corner that Vasquez could have clapped his revolver to the man's breast merely by stretching out his arm.

All this took half an hour. Then Carcante called out to the man in the launch, who came quickly and carried out various items.

Carcante took a last look at the cavern.

"Too bad we have to leave so much," said Vargas.

"We've got no choice. If only that schooner could take three hundred tons! But we've taken the most valuable stuff, and I've a hunch that where we're going we'll make the most of it!"

They left the cave, hoisted the launch's sail, and soon disappeared behind the tip of the bay.

Then it was Vasquez's turn to emerge and return to his grotto. In forty-eight hours he would have nothing left to eat. The sloop, assuming she arrived on schedule, was not due for another fortnight. When Kongre and his men left they would of course take all the supplies from the lighthouse, and Vasquez would find nothing at all.

This was a critical situation. Neither Vasquez's courage nor his energy could change it, unless he could feed himself by digging roots from the beech copse or catching fish in the bay. Even that would depend on the *Maule* leaving Staten Island for good. If for some reason she had to stay a few more days at her mooring, Vasquez would die of starvation in his grotto at Cape San Juan.

The day was getting on. The sky became more threatening, the winds from the sea stronger, and the gusts whipping the surface changed it into a powerful swell. Foam capped the crests of waves that would soon be breaking loudly over the rocks of the cape.

The schooner would surely not be able to leave on tomorrow's tide in such fierce weather.

Evening brought no change, and indeed things worsened. This was not a storm of two or three hours; a gale was coming on. All the indications were there: the color of the sky and sea, the disheveled clouds racing ever more swiftly, the tumultuous waves running headlong against the current and crashing onto the reefs. A sailor like Vasquez could read the signs, and in the lighthouse quarters he would have seen the barometer falling to below storm level.

In spite of the raging wind, Vasquez had not stayed in his grotto. He was pacing the beach, scanning the horizon as it steadily darkened. The last rays of the sun were fading on the opposite shore, but had not disappeared before Vasquez noticed a dark mass moving on the sea.

"A ship!" he exclaimed. "A ship! And apparently headed for the island!"

The ship was indeed coming from the east, intending to enter the strait or else pass to the south.

The storm now raged violently, no mere gale. It was the kind of irresistible hurricane that has proved to be fatal to the most powerful ships. Without "headway," to use the nautical term—that is, when land is to lee—it is rare indeed for any vessel to escape shipwreck.

"And the lighthouse! Those criminals have put it out!" bellowed Vasquez. "That vessel will look for it and see nothing! She has no way of knowing there's a coast a few miles away! The gales will push her and she'll break up on the reefs!"

The disaster he feared was of course due to Kongre's crew and their criminal machinations. Aloft in the lighthouse, they had surely noticed the ship carried along by the hurricane, unable to head back to the open sea on the angry billows and reduced to running before the wind. Vainly searching for the westerly lighthouse beacon, she could round neither Cape San Juan to enter Le Maire Strait nor Several Point to pass southward. In half an hour she would hit the reefs at the mouth of Elgor Bay.

Being wrecked was the only possible outcome. No lookout on this vessel could have any indication that land was close by, since there had been no chance to sight it before nightfall.

The storm came at its fiercest now. It would be a terrible night and a terrible morrow. There seemed no possibility that the hurricane would abate within the next twenty-four hours.

Vasquez did not think of heading back in, and his eyes never left the horizon. He could no longer make out the ship in the great darkness, although he could sometimes see her lights when she rolled back and forth in the impact of the monstrous waves, first on one side then on the other. She would never be able to respond to her helm when sailing at such a point. Her rudder was useless and she was probably helpless, having most likely lost one or more of her masts. In any case, her sails must be stowed, for she could hardly have kept a storm jib hoisted fore or aft when the elements raged so fiercely.

Vasquez knew the vessel was a sailing ship. He saw only green or red lights, and a steamer would have shown a white light on her mizzen stay. So she had no engine to help maintain her course.

Vasquez paced the shore, in despair that he could not prevent the shipwreck. Nothing could, short of a beacon from the lighthouse to dispel the darkness. Vasquez turned and glared towards Elgor Bay. He stretched out his arms uselessly. But the lighthouse was not going to shine out tonight, like every other night for almost two months. And the ship was fated to go down with all hands on Cape San Juan.

But an idea came to Vasquez. If the ship realized there was land here, it might still be possible for her to turn herself about or at least miss the island. Even if she found it impossible to tack, she could at least perhaps make a slight change in her heading. She might in that case avoid striking the shore, after all less than eight miles long between Cape San Juan and Several Point. After that, she would have the open sea ahead of her.

There was wood on shore, the remains of wrecks, the debris of their carcasses. Could he not carry some of it along to the point, pile it on a bed of dry seaweed, light a fire, and allow the wind to build up the flame? Would the fire not be seen from the vessel? And even if she were only a mile from the coast, might she not still have time to avoid it?

Vasquez set to work immediately. He picked up several pieces of wood and took them to the end of the cape. He had plenty of dry seaweed for, despite the raging wind, it had not yet begun to rain. When all was ready he attempted to light it.

Too late! An enormous mass emerged out of the darkness. It bore down with terrifying speed, then rose with the waves, and finally fell down on the reefs like an avalanche.

A horrifying din sounded a little to the left of the point, which sheltered Vargas from being buried under the debris from the wreck. A few cries of distress reached him amid the whistling of the wind, before being covered by the waves as they crashed over the rocky shore.

10. After the Wreck

Next day at sunrise, the storm still raged as furiously as ever.* The sea was entirely white to the furthest horizon. At the end of the cape, the waves frothed fifteen or twenty feet high; their foam spread in the wind and flew above the cliffs. At the mouth of Elgor Bay, the squalls clashed so violently with the descending tide that no boat could have come in or out. To judge from the sky, as threatening as ever, the storm was going to last a few days, which was not surprising in these Magellanic waters.

Quite clearly the schooner could not leave on such a morning, and it is easy to imagine the anger of Kongre and his gang at this setback.

Vasquez, rising at the crack of dawn amid the whirlwinds of sand, soon grasped the situation. This is what he saw:

The wrecked ship lay two hundred paces from him, where the shore doubled back beyond the cape, outside the bay, a three-master with a burden of about five hundred tons. Her three masts had been reduced to stumps, broken at the bases, either because the captain had been obliged to cut them in an effort to free the ship, or because they had toppled when she ran aground. In any case, no flotsam appeared on the surface; the force of the wind had perhaps pushed all the debris to the end of Elgor Bay. If so, Kongre must now be aware that a vessel had just been wrecked on the reefs of Cape San Juan.

Vasquez would have to be cautious. He ventured forth only after he had made sure that nobody from the gang was still at the mouth of the bay. In a few minutes he reached the site of the catastrophe. He went to the other side of the wrecked vessel and read on the transom of her stern: *Century*, Mobile.

So this sailing ship was American. Her home port was the capital of Alabama, one of the southern states of the Union, on the Gulf of Mexico.

The *Century* had been lost with all hands. No survivors could be seen and only a formless carcass remained. The collision had split the hull in two. The swell had carried off the cargo and dispersed it. The remains of planks, ribs, spars, and sheathing lay here and there on the reefs, beginning to emerge despite the sharp gusts. The tide had been going out two hours already. Boxes, cases, and barrels were spread out along the cape and beach.

Since part of the *Century* lay high and dry, Vasquez could enter both fore and aft. The devastation was complete. The waves had broken everything, stripped the planks off the deck, torn apart the cabins in the poop, demolished the forecastle, removed the helm—and hitting the reefs had completed the work of destruction.

And not an officer or crewman left alive.

"They all perished!" exclaimed Vasquez.

He shouted without a reply, then went below and found no bodies in the hold. The poor men had been either swept away by the wind or drowned when the *Century* crashed on the rocks.

Turning his eyes to the bay, Vasquez spotted two bodies, pushed by the wind towards the right bank near Several Point.

He went back to the beach to check that neither Kongre nor any of his companions were heading for the wreck. Then he retraced his steps against the wind along to the tip of Cape San Juan.

Maybe I'll find someone from the *Century* still breathing, and rescue him, he said to himself.

But his search was in vain, whether on the northern or southern side, or at the tip, where the sea raged in its all fury. Back on the beach, Vasquez set to examining the diverse items of flotsam washed ashore.

Perhaps I'll find some box of food to keep me going for a few weeks, he thought. And indeed, among the reefs he had soon found a keg and a box spared by the sea. They were labeled: the box held biscuits, the keg corned beef. So he had at least two months' bread and meat.

Then Vasquez, with one thought in his mind, said:

"May God prevent the schooner leaving and may the bad weather keep up until the relief arrives! Yes, make it so, God, and my poor comrades will be avenged!"*

First he carried the box to the grotto, a distance of at most a hundred paces, then rolled the keg to the same spot. Who could tell if this flotsam from the *Century* might not be carried away or broken on the reefs?

Vasquez came back to the corner of the cliff. He was sure that Kongre knew about the shipwreck. Aloft in the lighthouse before nightfall yesterday, he would have seen the ship heading for land. And now, given that the *Maule* could not sail off this morning, the gang would surely rush to the end of Elgor Bay. Would there not be something to salvage, perhaps some valuable objects? Would the looters let such an opportunity pass?

When he reached the corner, Vasquez felt surprised at the violence of the wind sweeping into the bay. The schooner could have made no headway against such a gale, and even if she had reached Cape San Juan she would never have been able to take to the open sea.

At that moment there came a brief calm, and he heard someone call, like a half-muffled voice crying out in pain. Vasquez ran in the direction of the voice, not far from the hole near the cavern where he had first taken refuge. After fifty paces at most he spotted a man lying at the foot of a rock. His hand was moving in an appeal for help.

In an instant Vasquez was beside the rock.

The man lying there looked between thirty and thirty-five. The sailor's uniform he wore was drenched. He lay on his right side, his eyes closed, his breath gasping, his body shaking with convulsive shudders. He did not seem to be wounded and no blood showed on his clothes.

This man, perhaps the only survivor from the *Century*, had not heard Vasquez approaching. When the latter put his hand on his chest he made a weak attempt to sit up, and fell back to the sand. But his eyes had opened for moment and these words escaped his lips:

"Help . . . help!"

Kneeling near him, Vasquez propped him up against a rock, carefully repeating:

"My friend, my friend! I'm here, look at me! I'll save you!"

All the wretch could do was stretch out his hand before losing consciousness. From his tremendous weakness it was clear he needed to be treated immediately.

"God grant me time!" said Vasquez.

The first task was to leave this spot. At any moment the gang could arrive in the launch or longboat, or even on foot following the left bank. Vasquez needed to immediately carry the man to the grotto for safety, and this is what he did. Taking the man's limp body on his back, he carried him the two hundred meters and through the rock fissure, a journey of about fifteen minutes, wrapped him in a blanket, and rested his head on a bundle of clothing.

The man was still unconscious, although breathing. He had no visible wound, but might have broken his arms or legs falling on the reefs. Since Vasquez would not have known what to do in such a case, the idea frightened him. Feeling and moving the man's limbs, his body seemed to feel whole.

Vasquez poured a little water into a cup, added the few drops of brandy still in his flask, and managed to loosen the man's lips enough to give him some. Then he changed the man's wet clothes for spare garments of his own, and rubbed his chest and arms.*

He could do nothing else. It was not hunger that had weakened this man, who the day before had been on board the *Century*.

The man was in the prime of life and of a vigorous constitution. At length Vasquez had the satisfaction of seeing that he was coming to. He even managed to sit up. Looking at Vasquez, who supported him in his arms, he said these words in a still weak voice:

"Water . . . water!"

Vasquez filled the cup and the man drank half of it.

"Do you feel better?" he asked.

"Yes . . . yes."

Agonizing memories still troubled the newcomer's mind.

"Here? . . . You? . . . Where am I?" he added, clasping his rescuer's outstretched hand.

He spoke in English. Vasquez, who knew the language, replied:

"You're safe. I found you on the beach after the wreck of the *Century*."

"The *Century*. Yes, I remember."

"What is your name?"

"Davis. John Davis."*

"The captain of the three-master?"

"No, first officer. And the others?"

"All lost," replied Vasquez. "Every last man. You're the only survivor from the wreck!"

"All of them?"

"All."

John Davis was thunderstruck. The only survivor! And it was due to mere chance! He understood he owed his life to the stranger who had just brought him to this grotto.

"Thank you. Thank you," he said, as a large tear fell from his eye.

"Are you hungry? Do you want something to eat? A little biscuit or meat?"

"No . . . no, more water!"

The fresh water mixed with brandy helped him immensely. Soon he gave replies to all of Vasquez's questions.

The following is, in brief, what John Davis said.

The *Century*, a three-masted sailing ship of 550 tons, from the port of Mobile, had left the American coast twenty days before. Her captain was Harry Steward and her first officer John Davis, in charge of a crew of twelve, including a cabin boy and a cook. She was making for Melbourne, Australia, with a cargo of nickel and trinkets. She had sailed the Atlantic without incident as far south as the fifty-fifth parallel. Then she ran into the violent storm that had been whipping these waters for twenty-four hours. No sooner had it begun than the *Century*, unprepared for such suddenness, had lost her mizzen mast and aft sails. After that an enormous wave had struck her port bow, swept the deck, and partly destroyed the poop. Two sailors were swept overboard, with no one able to rescue them.

Captain Steward's intention had been to follow Le Maire Strait. He felt certain of his latitude, having shot the sun that day. He assumed, quite reasonably, that this was the best way to round Cape Horn en route for the Australian coast.

The storm had increased during the night. All sails were taken in and reefed except the mizzen and mainsail, and the three-master sailed with the wind behind her.

The captain imagined he was still twenty miles from Staten Island, that there was no danger in continuing until he sighted the lighthouse. After that, following a west-southwest course in accordance with the coast guard instructions, he would run no risk of being thrown onto the reefs of Cape San Juan, and would be able to safely enter the strait.

So the *Century* continued to sail with the wind behind her. Harry Steward was confident of sighting the lighthouse within an hour, as its beacon would be visible over seven or eight miles.

Seeing no beacon, however, he still believed himself to be a good distance from the island. Then a terrifying collision happened. Three sailors, busy in the masts, disappeared with the mainmast as its base broke. At the same time, the hull split open and waves rushed in. The captain, the first officer, and the surviving crewmen were thrown overboard, where the undertow prevented anyone reaching safety.

Thus the *Century* had perished with all hands. Only First Officer John Davis had cheated death, thanks to Vasquez.

On what coast had the three-master been lost? This was what Davis couldn't understand, unless the *Century* had been at a lower latitude than Captain Steward thought. Had the hurricane thrown her on Tierra del Fuego, between Magellan and Le Maire Straits?

"Where are we?" he asked.

"On Staten Island."

"Staten Island!" exclaimed John Davis, stupefied.

"That's right," replied Vasquez. "At the mouth of Elgor Bay."

"But the lighthouse?"

"It wasn't lit."

Davis's face showed great astonishment. As he waited for Vasquez to continue, the lighthouse keeper started suddenly at a noise and rose to his feet. He wanted to be certain the Kongre gang had not arrived at the mouth of the bay.

So he slipped out between the rocks and surveyed the coast as far as the tip of Cape San Juan.

The shore was deserted, with waves still breaking with prodigious violence. The hurricane had lost none of its strength. Ever more threatening clouds hugged the horizon; fog obscured it less than two miles away.

What Vasquez had heard was the *Century* breaking apart. The impact of the wind had caused her aft section to turn over, and the gusts, penetrating the ship's interior, had pushed her further onto shore. Rolling like an enormous stove-in barrel, she had hit the cliff corner—and been utterly shattered. Of the three-master, only the forward part now remained, lying where she had been wrecked, covered with a myriad pieces of flotsam. Vasquez went back into the grotto and lay on the sand near John Davis. Strength was coming back to the *Century*'s first officer. If Vasquez had not stopped him, he would have been capable of rising and going down to the beach, supported on his companion's arm. Davis asked why there had been no lighthouse the night before.

Vasquez informed him of the terrible events at Elgor Bay seven weeks earlier.* For the twenty-two days following the departure of the sloop *Santa Fe*, the lighthouse had functioned uninterruptedly under Vasquez and his two colleagues Felipe and Moriz. Several vessels had passed the island during that time, and their signals had been acknowledged in the normal way.

At about eight in the evening of 2 January a schooner had appeared at the mouth of the bay. From his post in the lighthouse's lookout room, Vasquez saw her position lights. He assumed the captain must know the route to follow, since he did not deviate from it for an instant.

The schooner reached the inlet at the foot of the lighthouse perimeter, dropping anchor there.

It was then that Felipe and Moriz, who had left the quarters to offer the captain their help, went on board, only to be treacherously struck down and killed. They never had a chance to defend themselves.

"The poor fellows!" exclaimed John Davis.

"Yes! My poor companions!" repeated Vasquez, as his eyes filled with tears at the painful memory.

"And you?"

"From the top of the gallery I heard the cries of my colleagues, and I understood what had happened. It was a pirate ship, that schooner. There were three of us! They had killed two but did not worry about the third."

"How did you get away?"

"I ran down the lighthouse stairs and into the quarters. I took some food and things. I ran off before the crew of the schooner landed, and hid on this part of the shore."

"The criminals! The criminals! Now there's no beacon. So they're the ones who caused the wreck of the *Century* and the death of my captain and all our crew?"

"Yes, they've taken over the lighthouse. I overheard their leader talking with one of his men and found out what their plans were."

John Davis was told everything. These looters had been living on Staten Island for several years, luring ships into running aground before murdering the survivors. Then, while Kongre waited for a vessel he could seize, they had taken everything of value and hidden it in a cave. While the lighthouse was being built, the criminals had been forced to leave Elgor Bay and hide on Cape Gomez at the far end of Staten Island. No one had suspected they were there.

Once the lighthouse was finished, they came back. But by this time, they had taken over a schooner wrecked on Cape Gomez whose crew had perished.

"And when did the schooner arrive?"

"Thirty-two days ago."

"And she still hasn't left with the looters and their cargo?"

"They had to do a lot of repairs, and that stopped her until now. I was able to check for myself, Davis. She's finished loading and was due to leave this very morning."

"For . . .?"

"The Pacific islands. These bandits suppose they'll be safe there and can carry on their pirate trade."

"But the schooner can't leave until this storm is over?"

"No," replied Vasquez. "And it may last a whole week."

"And as long as they remain here, there's no lighthouse?"

"That's it."

"And other vessels may be lost like the *Century*?"

"Yes."

"If any ships approach this coast at night, couldn't we signal to them?"

"Maybe, by lighting fires. On this shore or the tip of Cape San Juan. That's exactly how I tried to warn the *Century*, Davis. A fire with some driftwood and dry grass. But the wind was blowing too hard."

"Well, Vasquez, what you couldn't manage alone, we'll accomplish together," declared John Davis. "We've got plenty of wood from my poor ship!* The point is that if the schooner can't leave, and if ships come here and can't see the Staten Island lighthouse, who knows what other shipwrecks may occur?"

"Whatever happens, Kongre and his gang can't stay on the island much longer, and the schooner'll leave as soon as the weather allows her."

"But why?"

"Because they know that the lighthouse crew are due to be relieved soon."

"When?"

"Early March. And today's 18 February."

"And a ship will come then?"

"Yes, the sloop *Santa Fe*, from Buenos Aires."

"Then," exclaimed John Davis, exactly as Vasquez had, "may this bad weather continue until that time! And may those criminals still be here when the *Santa Fe* anchors in Elgor Bay!"

11. The Wreckers

There they were, a dozen of them, Kongre and Carcante too, all drawn by the looting instinct.

The previous evening in the lighthouse gallery, just as the sun sank below the horizon, Carcante had sighted the three-master arriving from the east. As soon as Kongre was told, he deduced that the vessel was fleeing before the storm and trying to enter Le Maire Strait, to find shelter on the western coast of the island. Kongre continued to observe the ship as long as he could follow her course, and after nightfall could still see her lights. He soon realized that she was partly disabled and that she was about to run aground on a landfall whose existence she was unaware of. She would have been in no danger if the lighthouse had been lit, but Kongre had taken care that it was not. Then the *Century*'s lanterns went out, and Kongre knew the ship had been lost with all hands between Cape San Juan and Several Point.

The following day the hurricane continued to blow furiously, the schooner could not think of departing. That annoyed Kongre and his men, but they were faced with a few days' delay and they would just have to wait. After all it was only 18 February, and the storm would surely calm down before the end of the month. The instant the weather cleared, the *Maule* would weigh anchor and head for the high seas.

And in the meantime, since a vessel had now hit the coast, had they not got an opportunity to benefit from her destruction? Could they not enrich the schooner's cargo with whatever items they might find among the wreckage?

There was no point in even asking the question. These birds of prey spread their wings, so to speak, and flew as one. They swiftly prepared the launch, and about ten of them got on board with their leader. Their oars had to struggle mightily against a storm wind that drove the water into the bay, and it took them a good hour and a half to reach their destination among the cliffs. But the return journey would be quick thanks to the sail.

The launch landed on the left bank near the cavern. The crew disembarked and rushed to the site of the shipwreck.

At that moment their shouts interrupted John Davis's conversation with Vasquez, who took care not to be seen as he quickly crawled back to the grotto's mouth.

A moment later Davis had crept up beside him.

"Let me do this myself," Vasquez said; "you need rest."

"No, I want to see," replied John Davis. He was a man of energy, this first officer of the *Century*, as resolute as Vasquez, one of those iron-willed sons of America. His soul, as the popular saying goes, must have been bolted onto his body;* otherwise the two could never have held together when the three-master was wrecked.

By the same token he was an exceptional seaman. He had served as chief petty officer in the United States Navy before joining the merchant marine. Harry Steward had been due to retire as soon as the *Century* returned to Mobile, and her owners had chosen Davis himself to succeed as captain.

And of the ship he would soon have commanded, he could see only a formless mass of driftwood, now given over to a gang of looters!

If Vasquez's courage had needed restoring, this was the man to do it. But however determined and courageous this pair were, what could they accomplish against Kongre and his gang?

Raising their heads above the rocks, Vasquez and Davis observed the shore as far as Cape San Juan. Kongre, Carcante, and the others had stopped at the cliff angle, where the *Century*'s hull, shattered into pieces, had been flung by the hurricane at the foot of the cliff.

The looters were less than two hundred paces from the grotto, and their features could easily be distinguished. They were wearing oilskins, cinched at the waist to prevent the wind from blowing them about. They clearly had trouble resisting the force of the gale, and sometimes needed to buttress themselves against a piece of wreckage or rock to remain standing.

Vasquez recognized those he had seen on their first visit to the cavern, and was able to point them out to John Davis.

"The tall one," he said, "there, near the stern of the *Century*, is the one they call Kongre."

"The leader?"

"Right."

"And the man he's talking to?"

"Carcante, second-in-command. And from up there I saw one of those who struck down my comrades."

"Do you want to crack his skull?" said John Davis.

"Like a mad dog's."

It was nearly an hour before the looters had finished examining this part of the hull. They had foraged in every corner. The *Century*'s cargo of nickel was no use to them, and they planned to leave it on the beach, but perhaps they would find use for some of the trinkets on the three-master. They were soon seen transporting two or three boxes and as many bales, which Kongre set aside.

"If these thieves are looking for gold or silver, precious stones or money, they're not going to find a cent."

"They don't mind. They already have plenty in the cavern. The ships lost on these shores had some valuable stuff. What's on board that schooner, Davis, has to be worth a lot."

"And I can see why they're in such a hurry to make her safe and sound . . . but maybe their luck will run out—"

"Unless the weather changes," Vasquez observed.

"Or unless . . ."

John Davis did not finish his idea. After all, what could keep the schooner from sailing, once the storm was over, the weather moderate, and the sea calmer?

At that moment the looters abandoned the first half of the ship, and headed for the other part, lying where it had been wrecked, on the shore of Elgor Bay.

Vasquez and John Davis continued to survey them from their vantage point, albeit less clearly.

The tide was still going out. Although the wind was pushing back the water, the surface of the reef lay largely uncovered. The men easily reached the carcass of the three-master.

Kongre and two or three others climbed into the wreck. The ship's storeroom was aft, underneath the poop. John Davis was impatient to know what they would discover there.

The storeroom had very probably been damaged by the sheets of sea water that had continually hit it. But it seemed possible some of the supplies were still intact.

In fact several of the men came out with cases of food and kegs, which they rolled over the sand to the launch. The gang also took bundles of clothes from the remains of the poop and carried them along the beach.

In all they spent about two hours searching the ship. Then Carcante and two of his companions raised their axes and attacked the taffrail, about two or three feet from the ground because of the listing.

"What are they doing?" asked Vasquez. "Isn't the ship wrecked enough? Do they want to finish her off?"

"I guess," replied John Davis, "they want to destroy any sign of her name or nationality. They don't want anyone to know the *Century* was lost in this part of the Atlantic."

Davis proved right. A few moments later, Kongre had hauled down the American flag flying on the poop deck, and torn it into a thousand pieces.

"The criminals!" exclaimed John Davis. "The flag! The Stars and Stripes!"

He barely held back a cry of indignation, as if his very heart were being torn out. Vasquez had to grab his arm. Davis had lost control and was about to rush onto the beach!

Once the looting was over, with most of the results going into the launch, Kongre and Carcante came back up to the foot of the cliff. Vasquez and John Davis could hear them talking as they paced back and forth near the crack leading to the grotto.

"We can't leave tomorrow after all."

"I'm afraid the bad weather's going to last a few days."

"But we haven't wasted our time."

"Maybe not. But I hoped to find better in an American of this tonnage! The last one we pulled onto the reefs made us fifty thousand dollars."

"You win some, you lose some," replied Carcante.*

John Davis, exasperated, had seized Vasquez's revolver. He would have blown the gang leader's brains out if he had not been restrained in this moment of mindless anger.

"I'm sorry, you're right," said John Davis. "But I can't get used to these thugs getting away with it, and their schooner just being able to sail away! Then where to find them again? Where to even start looking?"

"The storm doesn't seem to be getting any better. If the wind starts up again, there'll be a stormy sea for several days more. Maybe they still won't be able to leave."

"But the sloop isn't supposed to arrive until early next month. Isn't that what you said?"

"Maybe earlier, Davis. Who knows?"

"May God decide, Vasquez. May God will it!"

Clearly the storm was losing none of its violence. At this latitude, such weather can last a fortnight, even in summer. If the wind turned southerly, it would bring humidity from the Antarctic, where winter would soon be arriving. Already the whalers would be planning to leave the polar seas, since new accretions begin to form around the pack ice as early as March.

Yet there was also danger that a calm would come in five or six days' time. The schooner would then leave.

It was four o'clock when Kongre and his companions boarded the launch, hoisted the sail, and a few moments later disappeared round the left bank.*

In the evening the gale strengthened. Buckets of cold biting rain poured out of the clouds coming from the southwest. Vasquez and John Davis were unable to leave the grotto. They lit a fire at the end of their passage to keep them from the freezing cold. With the shore deserted and the darkness complete, they feared nothing.

The night was terrible. The sea repeatedly struck the foot of the cliff. It was as if a tidal wave, or rather a tsunami, was attacking the east coast of the island. Surely a monstrous swell would reach the end of the bay, and Kongre would be hard put to keep the *Maule* at her mooring.

"I hope she's torn to splinters," John Davis kept saying, "and every single splinter washes out to sea on the next tide!"

Next day all that remained of the *Century*'s hull was fragments, caught between the rocks or scattered over the beach.

Had they seen the worst of the storm yet? Vasquez and his companion waited for dawn to bring the answer.

Far from it. Such a confounding of the waters of the sea and sky, such a chaos of elements, is impossible to imagine. There was no change either during the next day or night. Nor did any ship appear in sight; understandably, mariners wished at all costs to keep a safe berth from the perilous Magellanic lands, battered head-on by such tempests. Nowhere in Magellan or Le Maire Straits would they have found refuge from the assaults of this hurricane.

As John Davis and Vasquez had foreseen, the *Century*'s hull was entirely destroyed. A myriad bits of driftwood covered the shore as far as the rocks.*

Fortunately Vasquez and his companion did not need to worry about food. The supplies from the *Century* were sufficient for over a month. Before then, perhaps within ten days, the *Santa Fe* would hove in view. By then the stormy weather would be over, and she would not be afraid to sail close in to Cape San Juan.

The sloop was their most frequent topic. Vasquez indeed remarked:

"Let's hope the storm lasts long enough to keep the schooner from leaving, but short enough for the *Santa Fe* to get here!"

"If we could control the winds and the sea, we'd already have done it."

"Nobody but God can do that."

"And He won't want those criminals to go unpunished," concluded John Davis, using almost the same words as Vasquez. For the two were united in their thought—they felt the same hatred and the same thirst for revenge.

On the 21st and 22nd, the situation did not change, at least perceptibly. The wind might have veered slightly northeast, but its indecision lasted only an hour. It soon recovered its force and again visited its awesome gales on the island.

Not surprisingly neither Kongre nor any of his men had reappeared. No doubt they were busy protecting the schooner at her inlet, brimming with tides strengthened by the hurricane.

On the morning of the 23rd, the weather improved slightly. The wind hesitated and then stayed at north-northeasterly. The southern horizon cleared in places. The rain stopped, and although the wind was still blowing with violence, the sky gradually lightened. But the sea was still agitated, the waves breaking on shore as powerful as ever, and the mouth of the bay remained far from navigable. The schooner would not be able to sail for at least two days.

Kongre and Carcante might well take advantage of this slight calm to return to Cape San Juan to observe the condition of the sea. As this appeared not only possible but probable, John Davis and Vasquez took the necessary precautions.

They did not, however, fear a visit early in the morning, so ventured from the grotto for the first time in forty-eight hours.

"Will the wind hold?" Vasquez said immediately.

"Very likely," replied John Davis, whose sailor's instinct was seldom mistaken. "But what we need is ten days of foul weather. Ten days. And we're not going to get it."

His arms crossed, he looked at the sky and the sea. Since Vasquez had meanwhile moved a few paces away, he followed him along the foot of the cliff.

Suddenly Davis's foot hit a small metal box, half-buried in the sand near a rock. He bent over and found the box holding the powder for the *Century*'s firearms and for the cannon she used for signaling.

"Ah, we've got no use for it!" he exclaimed. "If only we could blow up the pirate schooner!"

"Don't even think about it," replied Vasquez, shaking his head. "Never mind. I'll take this box with me on the way back, and put it safely in the grotto."

They continued along the shore, heading for the cape whose tip they would be unable to reach. The force of the gales would see to that.

All of a sudden, having arrived at the reefs, Vasquez spotted in the hollow of a rock one of the little artillery pieces that had rolled there after the *Century* had run aground.

"This belongs to you. There's also some shot, which the waves brought here."

And John Davis repeated what he had said before: "We've got no use for it!"

"I don't agree," replied Vasquez. "Since we've now got some ammunition, we may have a chance to use it."

"Meaning?"

"Just this, Davis. There's no longer a beacon from the lighthouse. So if on some night a ship turns up as the *Century* did, couldn't we fire this cannon to warn them of the landfall?"

John Davis stared fixedly at his companion. Obviously an entirely different thought had occurred to him, but he merely replied:

"You really think so, Vasquez?"

"It's not a bad idea. Sure, they'd hear the explosion at the mouth of the bay, and they'd know we're on this part of the island. The bandits would start looking for us, and they might find us. It might cost us our lives, but we'd have done our duty."

"Our duty," repeated John Davis, and said no more.

As a result of the discussion, they dragged the cannon to the grotto, as well as its carriage and shot and the powder case. By the time Vasquez and John Davis returned for breakfast, the sun showed it to be about eight o'clock.

Scarcely had they got back before Kongre, Carcante, and the carpenter Vargas appeared round the cliff angle. It had presumably proved too difficult to row the launch against the wind, to say nothing of the tide that had begun to rise in the bay. They had made their journey on foot, following the left bank. This time they had not come for loot.

As Vasquez had guessed, the purpose of this visit was to observe the sky and sea in the improved weather conditions. They would of course realize the *Maule* still ran a great risk if she left the bay, and she could never have fought against the waves breaking in from the sea. True, she would only need to follow the strait in order to head west with the wind behind her. But first she would need to round Cape San Juan, where she would be in danger of running aground or at least being damaged by a very rough sea.

This was exactly what Kongre and Carcante thought. As they paused near the site of the shipwreck, where only debris remained of the *Century*'s bow, the wind made it difficult to remain standing.

They spoke excitedly, using gestures and pointing to the horizon, retreating whenever a foamy crest broke over the point.

Neither Vasquez nor his companion took their eyes off them during the half-hour they spent examining the mouth of the bay. Then, after turning to look back several times, they disappeared round the corner of the cliff and retraced their steps to the lighthouse.

"They've gone," said Vasquez. "I only hope they spend more days coming back to look at the sea off this island."

But John Davis shook his head. It was all too clear that the storm would be over in forty-eight hours and that the swells would have subsided, if not completely, then at least enough to allow the schooner to round Cape San Juan.

Vasquez and John Davis spent part of the day on the seashore. The change in the weather became marked. The wind blew steadily north-northeasterly, and it would not be long before a vessel could* navigate Le Maire Strait simply by reefing her mizzen and topsails.

As evening fell, Vasquez and John Davis went back to the grotto. They satisfied their hunger with biscuit and corned beef, their thirst with water mixed with brandy. Then Vasquez prepared to wrap himself in his blanket. His companion stopped him.

"Before we go to sleep, Vasquez, I'd like you to listen closely to something I have to say to you."

"Go on, Davis."

"Vasquez, I owe you my life and I don't want to do anything without your say so. I have a suggestion to make, so please just answer it and don't worry about offending me."

"I'm listening."

"The weather's changing. The storm's over. We're going to have a calm sea again. I expect the schooner to sail in forty-eight hours at most."

"Unfortunately, only too likely"—to this idea Vasquez added a gesture which meant: There's nothing we can do about it.

"Within two days she'll appear at the mouth of the bay. She'll sail out, round the cape, follow the strait, and disappear westward. We'll never see her again. Your comrades and my captain and shipmates from the *Century*—none will ever be avenged."

Vasquez had lowered his head. He raised it and looked at his companion, whose face was lit by the last gleams from the fire.

Davis continued:

"There's only one way to keep that schooner from leaving, and make her stay until the sloop arrives. Some damage that will force her back to the end of the bay. We've a cannon, we've gunpowder, and we've cannonballs. Let's mount this gun on its carriage, at the cliff angle. Let's load it. And when the schooner passes, let's fire straight at her hull. She may not sink with one shot, but any new damage will keep her from risking such a long voyage. She'll have to go back to anchorage for repairs. She'll have to unload her cargo, and it might take a week. And during that time, the *Santa Fe* . . ."

John Davis fell silent. He had seized his companion's hand.

Vasquez thought for a moment, then said:

"Do it!"

12. Leaving the Bay

The horizon was veiled with clouds on the morning of 25 February, as so often happens after a severe storm. But the wind fell as the sun rose higher, and a change in the weather was evident.

Today, it had been decided, the schooner would set sail, and Kongre made preparations to leave that afternoon. He considered it likely that the sun would dispel the mists in evidence that morning, and that the departure from Elgor Bay would be aided by the tide, due to begin going out at six in the evening. The schooner would round Cape San Juan at about seven, and the long dusk would allow her to reach Le Maire Strait before nightfall.

In fact only the fog prevented her from leaving on the morning tide. All was ready on board. The cargo had been loaded, along with abundant supplies from the *Century* and the lighthouse storerooms. All that remained in the annex were the kitchen items and the furniture, Kongre did not want to clutter up an already full hold. The ballast had been lightened, but the schooner was still a few inches below her normal burden. It would not have been sensible to exceed her water line any further.

Kongre had taken a further, very sensible precaution. The *Maule* was no longer called that, a potentially suspicious name even in the distant Pacific waters; he had given her the name of his second-in-command. The escutcheon below her stern now read *Carcante*, without any indication of home port.

Strolling inside the perimeter a little after midday, Carcante told Kongre:

"The fog is now rising. Before long we'll be able to see the open sea. These mists usually mean the wind falls and the tide goes out pretty fast."

"If you ask me, we'll get out this time. Nothing will get in the way of sailing over the strait."

"But it's going to be a dark night, Kongre. It's hardly the first quarter of the moon yet, and that crescent's going to vanish soon after sunset."

"It doesn't matter, Carcante. I don't need any moon or stars to sail along this island. I know the north coast like the back of my hand. And when I go around Parry Point, I'm planning to be far enough from shore to stay clear of those rocks."

"And by tomorrow we'll be miles away, Kongre. With a north-easterly sea wind in our sails."

"Before tomorrow's an hour old, we'll be out of sight of Cape Gomez. With any luck, Staten Island'll be forty miles astern!"

"And not a day too soon, Kongre, after the three years we've—"

"Any regrets, Carcante?"

"Not after making our fortunes, as they say. And a fine ship to take us out of here, money and all! But the devil if I didn't think we were done for when the *Maule*—I mean the *Carcante**—came sailing into the bay with her leak! If we hadn't been able to fix it, who knows how long we'd have been stuck on this island? And we'd have needed to get back to Cape Gomez before that sloop arrived—"

"In fact," said Kongre, and his cruel features darkened, "it would have been worse than that. The Santa Fe's captain would have swung into action as soon as he saw the lighthouse keepers were gone. He'd have started searching the whole island, and who knows if he wouldn't have found our hideout? And he might have met up with that third keeper we didn't catch."

"No problem there, Kongre. We didn't see any sign of him. Anyway, how was he supposed to live for nearly two months with no food? That's how long the *Carcante*'s been lying in Elgor Bay—I didn't forget her new name this time! And unless our friend the lighthouse keeper's been living on roots and raw fish all this time—"

"Anyway, we'll be out of here before the sloop gets back. It's better like that."

"According to the ledger, she's not due for another week."

"And in a week we'll be far from Cape Horn, on our way to the Solomons or the New Hebrides."

"Right. I'm just going up to the gallery to take one last look at the sea, and check there's no vessels in sight."

"Who cares!" said Kongre with a shrug. "Since when has the Atlantic or Pacific been anybody's private property? The *Carcante*'s papers are in order. And what if she does run into the *Santa Fe* right at the mouth of the strait? Fire a salute and dip your colors!"

Clearly Kongre was confident his plans would succeed. And it did seem that everything was favoring him.

As the chief went back down to the inlet, Carcante climbed the lighthouse stairs, where he spent the next hour watching from the gallery.

The sky was quite clear now, and the horizon stood out very sharply, twelve miles out. The sea still moved, but white horses were now absent. However high the swells, they could not impede the schooner's progress. At any rate she would enjoy fine sailing as soon as she hit the strait.

Out to sea no ships apart from a lone three-master. She appeared to eastward at about two o'clock, very briefly and at such a distance that Carcante could not make out her sails without a telescope. She was sailing south, so was obviously not heading for the Pacific. She had soon disappeared.

An hour later, however, Carcante did have cause for worry, and found himself wondering whether or not to alert Kongre.

A column of smoke appeared in the north-northeasterly distance. A steamer was bearing down on the island as she followed the coast of Tierra del Fuego.

And now a sudden fear entered Carcante's mind: Might it be the sloop? But today was only 25 February, and the *Santa Fe* was not due until the beginning of March. So had she left ahead of schedule? If it was her, she would be off Cape San Juan within two hours, and all was lost.

For although the schooner had only to raise anchor to be on her way, an unfavorable wind would have prevented her overcoming the tide, already beginning to rise. The sea would not turn until half past two, and the schooner couldn't possibly sail before the steamer got here. If it really was the sloop . . .

But Carcante decided not to disturb Kongre, who would be busy with the final preparations. Instead, he continued his solitary vigil.

The current and the wind assisted the vessel's swift approach. Her captain was making all steam. Thick smoke emerged from the funnel, still invisible to Carcante behind the straining sails. The ship was listing strongly to port. She would soon be off Cape San Juan, then in the strait, then at the southeastern tip of Tierra del Fuego.

Carcante, eye glued to telescope, felt his anxiety increasing as the steamer neared; soon she was only a few miles away, and part of the hull was in view. At this point his fears were at their maximum. But no sooner had he decided to warn Kongre than his worry disappeared.

The steamer had just turned about and caught the wind abeam, showing she wished to enter the strait. Carcante could now see her rigging. She was indeed a steam vessel, probably of burden of 1,200 to 1,500 tons, and could never have been confused with the *Santa Fe*.

Kongre and his cronies knew the sloop well, having seen her several times at the mouth of Elgor Bay. They knew that she was rigged as a schooner, whereas the approaching steamer was a three-master.*

Greatly relieved, Carcante congratulated himself on not disturbing gang's peace of mind. He stayed in the gallery for another hour, long enough to see the steamer pass into the strait, three or four miles out to sea. At such a distance she could not have sent a signal, which in any case Carcante would have had good reason to ignore.

Forty minutes later the steamer, steaming at twelve knots, vanished off Parry Point.

Carcante then went down again, after making sure that no other ship was approaching these waters.

It was almost time for the tide to turn and the schooner to depart. All was ready and the sails were about to be hoisted. Once they were hauled in taut, having caught the wind abeam, the *Carcante* would make for the open sea, keeping to the middle of the bay.

By six o'clock, Kongre and most of the men were on board. The longboat was hoisted and secured, having brought back those waiting below the lighthouse perimeter.

The tide slowly ebbed, partly uncovering the spot where the *Maule* had rested in the sand for the repairs. Across the inlet rose the rocks with their jagged heads. The wind pierced the cliff faces as a slight undertow washed the foot of the perimeter.

It was time to leave. Kongre gave the order to haul on the capstan. The cable tightened and grated on the hawse. When the anchor was apeak, all was ready for a long voyage.

The sails were trimmed, and the schooner—under her mizzen, mainsail, topsail, topgallant, and jib—sailed out between the shores of the bay.

Since the *Carcante* was sailing at broad reach, the wind would tend to drive her south. This would take her into the open sea off Cape San Juan, at least a mile away, for the bay had these dimensions from one cape to the other. But the reefs were very dangerous in that direction, stretching under the surface, and it was prudent to keep a certain distance out.

Kongre was aware of this; he knew the bay well. As he stood at the helm, he did not allow the schooner to luff. He would thus round Cape San Juan close in, for its rocks protruded only a few fathoms into the deep water.*

In short, the schooner made halting progress. She slowed down when the tall cliffs sheltered her, but speeded up when the wind swept in across a more open area. She advanced ahead of the tide and left a relatively flat wake.

At half past six, Kongre found himself a mere mile and a half from the mouth of the bay. He saw the sea stretching out to meet the sky. In the opposite direction, the sun was setting, and a few stars shone at the zenith, darkening under the veil of dusk.

Carcante came up to him and said:

"At long last we're almost out of the bay!"

"Twenty minutes to go. I'll tighten the sheets to round Cape San Juan."

"Should we tack to the mouth of the strait?"

"Probably not. We'll go to leeward and as close to the wind as we can. Then in the strait we'll go about, then to broad reach, and head for Parry Point."

Kongre's wish was to avoid tacking while leaving the bay, to gain an hour. He was confident of making it, for the schooner sailed well at all points. If necessary he could even strike the square sails, and retain only the lateen sails, the spanker, foresail, and jibs, since the strait was only three miles off.

Suddenly a crewman near the bow cried out:

"Look out! Dead ahead!"

"What is it?" demanded Kongre.

Carcante ran up to the man and leaned over the rail.

"Bear away!" he shouted to Kongre. "Handsomely!"

The schooner was at that moment off the cave that had long been the gang's hideout.

Part of the *Century*'s keel was drifting in this area of the bay, and the tide was pushing it out to sea. If the schooner hit the keel, it might cause serious damage, which it was urgent to avoid.

Kongre turned the wheel slightly to port. The schooner changed course and passed the keel, which merely grazed her hull.

Her maneuver sent her a little off the left bank,* but she quickly resumed her course. Twenty fathoms later, she would pass the cliff corner and the wind would hit her sails.

All of a sudden, a loud explosion happened and the air whistled. Something hit the schooner's hull, and she shook with the impact.

At the same time whitish smoke rose above the corner of the cliff, which the wind pushed towards the center of the bay.

"What the devil was that?" exclaimed Kongre.

"An attack," replied Carcante.

"Take the helm!"

Rushing to port, he looked over the rail. A hole gaped in the schooner's hull, about a foot above the water line.

The entire crew had moved forward to this side of the schooner. An attack from that part of the shore! The *Carcante* had received a cannonball in her flank, just as she was setting out—a shot that would have sunk her if it had hit a little lower! Such an assault, it must be agreed, was cause for astonishment and anxiety.

What could Kongre and his companions do? Break out the longboat, land it on the bank where the smoke had appeared, seize those who had fired, and kill them or at least drive them away? But could they be sure these attackers did not outnumber them? And was it not best to retreat now and check the extent of the damage?

That such was the best course of action seemed all the more obvious when the cannon fired again. Swirls of smoke appeared at the same place as before. The schooner felt another impact. A second cannonball hit broadside, a little behind the first.

"Hard up helm!" screamed Kongre. He ran aft to find Carcante, who executed his order double haste.

As soon as the schooner felt the wheel turning, her sheets were eased and in less than three minutes she was half a mile from the left bank, out of reach of the artillery that threatened her.

In fact, no further explosion sounded. The shore remained deserted as far as the end of the cape. Evidently there would be no more attacks.

The most urgent was to check the condition of the hull. They could not check the interior, because they would have needed to move the cargo. But what seemed certain was that both cannonballs had pierced the ship's planking and lodged in the hold.

While the *Carcante*, disabled, drifted only with the ebb tide, they struck the longboat. Kongre and the carpenter immediately climbed aboard and went to examine the hull to see if the damage might be repaired on the spot.

Two cannonballs had hit the schooner and entirely punctured the ship's frame. Fortunately the interior of the *Carcante* had been spared, and both holes were located above the copper lining and the flotation line. A foot lower, and the crew might not have had time to repair the leak. The hold would have filled up, and the *Carcante* would surely have sunk at the mouth of the bay. Of course Kongre and his companions could have escaped to shore in the boat, but the schooner would have been lost for good.

All in all the damage did not appear very serious. But it would surely prevent the *Carcante* from venturing further out to sea, for as soon as she began to list to port, her interior would be flooded. For the voyage to continue it was imperative, then, to plug both cannonball holes.

"But who did this to us?" Carcante kept repeating.

"Maybe that lighthouse keeper we didn't catch," replied Vargas. "And maybe also some survivor of the *Century*. Perhaps that keeper rescued him—"

"And the cannon," added Carcante, "must have come from the three-master. Too bad we didn't find it ourselves among the wreckage—"

"That doesn't matter," Kongre interrupted brusquely. "What matters is fixing the damage fast!"

Obviously, the task at hand was not to discuss how the attack had happened but to repair the harm. It would only take half an hour to sail the *Carcante* near the opposite shore of the bay at Diegos Point. True, she would be too exposed there to sea winds, and this coast offered her no shelter as far as Several Point; at the first bad weather she would break up on the reefs. So Kongre's view was that they must return that very evening to the end of Elgor Bay. There they could work in complete safety and with all due haste.

At present, however, the tide was ebbing, and the schooner could not have gained against it. They had to wait until three o'clock, when the tide would turn.

The *Carcante* was rolling with the swell, and the drifting might have carried her as far as Several Point or waterlogged her. Kongre had to resign himself to dropping anchor a cable length from Diegos Point.

The situation seemed distressing. Night was falling, and the darkness would be deep. It would take all of Kongre's know-how to prevent the *Carcante* from being wrecked on one bank or the other.

Finally, at about ten o'clock, the tide turned* and the anchor was raised. Before midnight, having run so many dangers, the *Carcante* had returned to her old mooring in the inlet of Elgor Bay.

13. Two Days

It is easy to imagine the exasperation of Kongre, Carcante, and the others.* To be stopped at the last moment, just when they were about to leave the island for good! And in four or five days, the sloop might appear off Elgor Bay . . .!* If only Kongre had known of a different mooring, on the northern or southern coast, he would certainly have steered the schooner there. But in a northerly wind, could he have succeeded . . .? The *Carcante* would have needed to take a starboard tack in the strait and along the south coast, so listing to port and causing water to flow into the cannonball holes. Several Point was only a few miles away, but to anchor there would require a cove suitable for mooring, and he knew that no such cove existed. Returning to the lighthouse had been his only option.

Hardly any of the crew slept that night. Instead they kept watch and guarded the approach to the inlet. Might there be another attack . . .? Was it possible that some force, perhaps larger than Kongre's gang, had landed elsewhere on the island? Had word of the pirate band finally reached Buenos Aires, and were the Argentine government attempting to eliminate them . . .?

Kongre and Carcante sat astern and discussed the situation. Or rather the latter spoke for both, for the chief was too absorbed to reply with more than a few words.

Carcante suggested that perhaps a detachment had landed on Staten Island in pursuit of Kongre and his gang, but had to admit that, even if such a landing had happened without their knowledge, an ambush would not have been carried out in this way. Any military force would have placed several vessels at the mouth of the bay to block the schooner's route—thus making sure she could not continue—before pursuing and seizing her that very evening.

So Carcante abandoned his theory, and took up the one he and Vargas had already formulated.

"Whoever who fired that shot did it to keep the schooner from leaving the island. If there are several of them, then some of the *Century*'s crew must have survived. They probably met up with that lighthouse keeper, and he told them what was going on. He must have also told them the sloop was coming soon."

"But that sloop isn't here yet," said Kongre. His voice shook with anger. "And before she is, this schooner'll be miles away!"

This was in fact very likely. Granting that the keeper had met the shipwreck survivors, there could only have been two or three of them, and they would be powerless against an armed gang of about fifteen. And once the schooner was repaired, she would sail again for the open sea, this time following the right bank of the bay. What had happened once must not happen again.

So it was merely a question of time. How many days would it take to repair the new damage . . .?

No alarm sounded that night. Next day, the crew set to work. Their first task was to move the portion of the cargo stored against the port flank of the hull. Moving such a load onto deck took a whole half-day. It would not, of course, be necessary to unload the cargo, or to bring the schooner about on the sandbank; the holes from the cannonball were located above the water line, and the men could easily patch them using the longboat, bringing it alongside the flank. The essential thing to ascertain was that the cannonballs had not damaged the ship's rib.

So Kongre and the carpenter went down into the hold, and this is what they discovered. The two cannonballs, which they found in the hull, had only just touched the planks and grazed the frame, whose structure had not been weakened. The openings of the holes, two and a half feet apart, were quite clean; a pair of plugs, kept in place with a wooden slab inserted in the rib beneath a sheet of sheathing, would suffice to make them watertight.

In short the damage was not great, its impact on the condition of the hull minimal, and it could soon be fixed.

"When?" asked Kongre.

"I'll get the piece of wood ready and put it in position this afternoon," replied Vargas.

"And the plugs . . .?"

"I'll cut them tomorrow morning and fix them in the evening."

"So we can sail tomorrow night?"

"No problem."

In sum forty-eight hours would suffice for the repairs, and the *Carcante*'s departure would be delayed only two days.

But Kongre decided to wait one more day before raising anchor. Vargas asked why.

"Because I plan to follow the right bank. I don't want us to get too close to the cliff and catch another ball. But I don't know the right bank so well, and we need darkness if we're going to follow it. The evening tide comes late, eight at the earliest. I'm not going to risk running the schooner onto those rocks."

Clearly this was more sensible. The man certainly possessed intelligence. Alas, he used it only to evil ends.

Carcante then asked him if he had considered visiting Cape San Juan "to see what's going on over there, in either the morning or afternoon."

"What for? We don't even know who we're up against. We'd need ten or twelve men, and there'd be only two or three left to guard the schooner. Who knows what might happen while we were gone?"

"That makes sense," admitted Carcante. "Anyway, what would we get out of it? The important thing is to leave this island—"

"We'll be at sea the morning of the day after tomorrow."

All in all, there was no reason to believe the sloop would be sighted before their departure, since she was not due until the end of the first week of March.*

And even if Kongre and his companions had gone to Cape San Juan, they would have found no trace of Vasquez or John Davis.

This is what had happened: John Davis's idea had kept them busy until the previous evening. They had decided to position the artillery right at the corner of the cliff. It was a simple enough task for Vasquez and John Davis to set up the gun carriage among the rocks at this angle. Moving the cannon there, however, did require considerable effort. First they needed to drag it over the sandy shore and then raise it using levers to cross a rocky area where dragging was out of the question. All this was both slow and fatiguing.

It was nearly six o'clock before the cannon had been set on its carriage and aimed at the mouth of the bay. Next John Davis proceeded to load it with a heavy charge of powder, packed in with a stuffing of dried kelp and completed with the cannonball. Next he readied the priming hole, so that it only remained to light it at the desired moment.

John Davis had said:

"I've been thinking about what we need to do. Sinking the schooner would be pointless. Those criminals would all just come ashore, and we might not be able to get away from them.* The important thing is to force the schooner back to the mooring, and stay there to repair the damage—"

"Maybe," remarked Vasquez. "But repairing a hole only takes a morning—"

"No, because they'll have to move the cargo. I estimate forty-eight hours at least. And it's already 28 February."

"But what if the sloop takes a week to arrive . . .?" rejoined Vasquez. "Wouldn't it be better to hit the masts than the hull?"

"Of course it would. I don't see how they could replace their mizzen and mainmast if we disabled them, and the schooner would be stuck at the end of that bay for quite some time. But a mast is harder to hit than a hull. We need to make sure our shots reach their target."

"Yes, and if those criminals leave only on the evening tide, as they probably will, it'll already be getting dark. Do what you think best, Davis."

Everything was ready. Vasquez and his companion had only to wait. They took up position beside the cannon, ready to fire as soon as the schooner passed.

We already know what happened when the cannon was fired, and how the *Carcante* was obliged to sail back to her mooring. John Davis and Vasquez did not leave their post until seeing her retrace her course along the left bank.

Now they needed to find a safe hideout on some other part of the island. For as Vasquez had said, Kongre and some of his cronies might decide to return in the launch to Cape San Juan next day, looking for them. But they had the whole night to think about this, and they spent it in the grotto without the alarm being sounded.

Next morning they had made up their minds: they would leave the grotto and search for another, a mile or two away and nearer the strait, where they could spot any ship arriving from the north. If the *Santa Fe* appeared, they would head back to Cape San Juan and signal her. Captain Lafayette would send a boat to take them aboard, and they would explain the situation to him. Things would finally be resolved, whether the schooner still lay in the inlet or had already sailed, which was unfortunately possible.

"God forbid," John Davis and Vasquez kept repeating.

At dawn, the two men took food, weapons, and blankets and followed the shore for about three miles. After a few searches, they found a hollow at the foot of the cliff, which would be enough to shelter them until the sloop arrived. In any case, if the schooner did set sail they would be able to return to their grotto.

That day Vasquez and John Davis remained on guard. Since the tide was still coming in, they knew the schooner could not leave the bay, and so did not worry. But before the turn of the tide, they felt again their old fear that the repairs might have been finished during the night. And surely Kongre would not delay his departure even for an hour. How he must dread the sight of the *Santa Fe*, as much as John Davis and Vasquez longed for it with every ounce of their beings!

Meanwhile they kept watch on the shore. But neither Kongre nor any of his companions showed themselves.

As we know, Kongre had decided not to make any such excursion, perhaps fruitless. His aim was to commence the task and finish the repairs as soon as possible, which is exactly what he did. Just as Vargas the carpenter had said, the piece of wood was positioned within the rib in the afternoon. Next day the holes would be plugged, and the *Carcante* could have sailed on the evening tide. But as we also know, Kongre planned to delay raising anchor until the following day.

So on this first day of March, Vasquez and John Davis received no alarm. But how long the day seemed to them!

That evening, after watching for any signs of the schooner's departure, and having satisfied themselves she had not left her mooring, they bedded down in their hollow, where sleep gave them much-needed rest.

They rose at dawn, and immediately looked out to sea. No ship in sight. The *Santa Fe* had not appeared, and no smoke was visible on the horizon. Would the schooner set sail now? The tide had turned, and by taking advantage of it she might round Cape San Juan within an hour.

John Davis did not dream of repeating the previous day's attempt. Kongre was a cautious man. When he sailed past, he would be out of range, and the cannonballs would fall short of the schooner.

It is easy to imagine what impatience and anxiety weighed John Davis and Vasquez down until the tide had gone out. But at last, towards seven o'clock, it began to rise again. Now Kongre would be unable to set out until the next evening's tide.

It was fine weather. The wind stayed northeasterly, and the sea had forgotten the last storm. The sun shone through the very high light clouds, above the reach of the wind.

It seemed another interminable day for Vasquez and John Davis. As on the previous day, there was no alarm. The gang did not leave the inlet, and it appeared quite improbable they would visit Cape San Juan during the morning or afternoon.

"It proves those rascals are hard at work—"

"Yes. They're not wasting any time," replied John Davis. "The cannonball holes will soon be patched . . . and there'll be nothing to keep them here."

"Maybe tonight . . . although it's a late tide," added Vasquez. "They certainly know the bay. They don't need light to show their way . . . Yesterday they sailed in after dark . . . If they set out tomorrow night, they'll be gone."

"What a disaster!" exclaimed John Davis. "If only I'd hit her mast . . .!"

"What can you expect, Davis? We did everything we could. The rest is in God's hands."

John Davis became pensive. He paced the beach, his eyes turned north. Nothing was on the horizon . . . nothing!

Suddenly he stopped, came back to his companion, and said:

"Vasquez, why don't we go and see what they're up to?"

"At the end of the bay, Davis?"

"We'll see if the schooner's finished or getting ready to leave."

"What good will that do?"

"We'll *know*, Vasquez!" exclaimed John Davis. "I'm burning with impatience! I can't take it any more."

"Calm down, Davis."

"I can't. It's stronger than me!"

And it was true. The first officer of the *Century* was no longer in control.

"Vasquez, how far to the lighthouse?"

"No more than three or four miles as the crew flies: you just follow the cliff and then the plateau to the end of the bay."

"Well I'm going, Vasquez . . . I'll leave at about four and get there before six. I'll slip along to the plateau . . . It'll still be daylight . . . They won't see me, but I'll see them."

Vasquez realized that John Davis was not to be dissuaded, and when his companion said "You stay here and watch the sea . . . I'll be back in the evening . . . I'll go alone" Vasquez responded, "I'm going with you, Davis."

It was decided. So, at four o'clock, having eaten some biscuit and corned beef, the two men set off, armed with their revolvers.

From a narrow valley they had easy access to the cliff top, which they reached without too much difficulty.

Before them stretched a broad dry plateau, with only a few barberry thorn clumps and not a tree in view. A few flocks of seabirds fled southward with deafening cries.

The route to the end of Elgor Bay was clear.

"That way!" said Vasquez.

And he pointed to the lighthouse, standing four miles away across the plateau.

"Let's go!" replied John Davis.

And the two set off at a rapid pace. Once they got near the inlet, it would be time for caution.

Only after half an hour did they stop to catch their breath. Neither felt any fatigue—although John Davis had dragged Vasquez along as if holding his hand.

They still had a mile to do. Caution was now required, for Kongre or one of his men might be on watch, and so spot them from the lighthouse gallery.

The clear sky made the gallery easily visible, even at this distance, and it was unoccupied. But if Carcante or someone else was in the duty room, he would be able to look through the narrow windows, which commanded a view of the four cardinal points, and see the entire plateau.

John Davis and Vasquez slipped through the profusion of scattered boulders, sometimes creeping from one rock to another across open spaces. Their progress was much slower for this last mile.

It was nearly six o'clock when they reached the cliff top above the inlet. In the last glimmers, both crawled to the very edge and cast their eyes below.

No one could have seen them here unless one of the gang had climbed the cliff. Even from atop the lighthouse, they would be invisible among the rocks.

The schooner lay there in the inlet, her mast and yards ready for the voyage, her tackle shipshape. The deck was free of the part of the cargo presumably placed there during the repair of the hull's interior. The longboat no longer floated against the port flank, but was fastened astern, indicating that work was finished and that the cannonball holes had been repaired.

"They're ready," muttered John Davis. He was holding in his anger, on the point of exploding.

"Who knows? Maybe they'll set sail on the tide, in two or three hours' time . . ."

"And we can do nothing. Nothing at all."

Vargas the carpenter had been as good as his word. He had worked quickly and efficiently, and no trace of the damage remained. These two days had sufficed. The cargo was back in place, the leaks patched, and the *Carcante* ready to set out.*

Had it not been for Kongre's reasoning, the crew would have raised anchor at about eight o'clock to catch the descending tide. Shortly after nine, the schooner would have rounded Cape San Juan. Then the sea, the guarantor of her freedom, would have opened wide before her.

Vasquez recognized Kongre clearly as he strolled around the perimeter with Carcante. A few of the men were still on land, the others on board.

Kongre spoke with his companion for a quarter of an hour. When they separated Carcante headed for the annex door.

"Careful!" said Vasquez in a low voice. "He's probably going into the lighthouse. He mustn't see us!"

The two men slipped further into the shelter of the rocks. Carcante was, in fact, going up the stairs one last time. The schooner would depart on the morning's high tide. He wanted to observe the horizon and see whether any vessel might be coming in sight of the island.

It was going to be a calm night. The wind had died down with evening, which promised fine weather at sunrise.

John Davis and Vasquez saw Carcante clearly as he reached the gallery. He walked round it, his telescope at his eye, examining every point of the horizon.

Suddenly a cry escaped from his mouth. Kongre and the others looked up at him. All could hear him screaming:

"The sloop! The sloop!"

14. The Sloop *Santa Fe*

How to describe the agitation at the end of the bay? This cry "Sloop . . . sloop!" had rung out like a thunderclap, like a death warrant on these thugs. The *Santa Fe* represented justice reaching the island, she presaged the punishment for so many crimes they would no longer be able to flee!

But had Carcante made a mistake? Was the ship approaching really the Argentine Navy sloop? Was this not simply a vessel heading for Le Maire Strait or Several Point and the south of the island? Was her destination really Elgor Bay?

As soon as Kongre heard Carcante he rushed back to the enclosure, to the lighthouse staircase, and up to the gallery in less than two minutes.

"Where is that ship?" he asked.

"There . . . north-northeast."

"How far?"

"Five or six miles."

"So she can't reach the mouth of the bay before nine o'clock?"

"No."

Kongre took the telescope and observed the vessel very carefully without a word.

There could be no doubt it was a steamer. Her smoke could be made out even at this distance and her hull was just coming into view. Nor could there be any doubt she was forcing her fires to reach the mouth of Elgor Bay before nightfall.

And nor could Kongre or Carcante hesitate to identify this steamer as the sloop. During the construction work they had seen her several times as she was rejoining or leaving these shores. Also, the steamer was heading directly for Staten Island. If the captain had intended to enter Le Maire Strait he would have set course to west and not southwest.

"Yes," Kongre finally said, "it *is* the sloop!"

"Blasted ill-luck has kept us here until now!" exclaimed Carcante. "Without those bastards we'd already be in the heart of the Pacific."

"It's no use saying that now," Kongre shot back. "We need to decide."

"What?"

"To cast off."

"When?"

"At the turn of the tide."

"But by then the sloop will be abeam of the bay."

"Yes, but still outside."

"Why?"

"Because she won't see the light from the lighthouse and in the dark won't risk venturing as far as the inlet."

This eminently logical reasoning of Kongre's was also being made by John Davis and Vasquez. They refused to leave as long as they might be seen from the gallery. But they talked together in low voices saying exactly the same as Kongre. The lighthouse should have been lit because the sun had just disappeared below the horizon. And not seeing the light, although he had probably sighted the island, would Captain Lafayate not think twice about continuing on his way? Unable to explain the darkness, would he not stay outside the bay all night? He had already come into Elgor Bay ten times, but only in daytime, and without the lighthouse to show his way he would surely not risk crossing the dark bay. Also he must think something serious had taken place on the island since the keepers were not at their post.

"But," said Vasquez, "if the captain did not sight the land, which is quite low, if he continues sailing in the hope of seeing the light, might the same thing not happen to him as the *Century*: being wrecked on the reefs of Cape San Juan?"

John Davis did not reply. It was only too true—what Vasquez said might easily happen! The wind was undoubtedly not of gale force and the *Santa Fe*'s circumstances were not the same as the *Century*'s. But a tragedy could be in the offing all the same.

"Let's run to the shore," pursued Vasquez. "We'll reach the cape in two hours and perhaps have time to light a fire to indicate land."

"No, it'd be too late as the sloop'll reach the mouth of the bay in about an hour."

"What can we do then?"

"Wait!"

It was seven o'clock and dusk had begun to creep over the island.

Meanwhile the preparations for the *Carcante*'s departure continued apace. Kongre wanted to sail at all costs. Although he knew he could not beat the *Santa Fe* to the mouth of the bay, he thought she would stay outside and cruise on the open sea waiting for daylight. Eaten up with worry, Kongre resolved to leave his mooring immediately. If he sailed only on the morning tide he risked meeting the sloop. On seeing the schooner, Captain Lafayate would not let her pass. He would order her to stop, he would question the captain. He would clearly want to know why the lighthouse had not been lit. The *Carcante*'s presence would rightly seem suspicious to him. When she had stopped he would go on board, he would call Kongre, inspect his crew, and just from their faces he would have the most justified suspicions. He would make them tack about and follow him, and would keep them in the inlet until he had more information.

And then, when the *Santa Fe*'s captain failed to find the three lighthouse keepers, he could only explain their absence by some sort of attack on them. Would he not deduce the perpetrators had to be the men of this ship trying to slip away?

And there might be other complications. Since Kongre and his gang had spotted the *Santa Fe* off the island, was it not probable, certain even, that she had been seen by the man or men who the day before yesterday attacked the *Carcante* just as she was leaving? They presumably watched all the sloop's movements and would be there when she arrived in the inlet. If, as could be thought, the third keeper was among them, Kongre and his men would no longer escape punishment for their crimes.

Kongre had glimpsed all these possibilities and their consequences. Accordingly he had decided on the only possible course of action: to set sail there and then without waiting for the outgoing tide, to try to overcome the current of the bay by cracking on more sail, since the north wind would be favorable, and thus reach the open sea under cover of night. Then the schooner would have the ocean before her. The sloop might easily be at that moment some distance away from Staten Island and unable to sight the lighthouse, if the captain had not wished to get too close in the darkness. And if necessary, as an extra precaution, instead of heading for Le Maire Strait, Kongre could sprint south round Several Point and hide behind the southern coast. So he took measures to sail as soon as possible.

Aware of what was going to happen, John Davis and Vasquez wondered how they could prevent this plan from succeeding—and with despair realized their utter helplessness!

At about half past seven Carcante called the last few men still on dry land. As soon as the crew were on board, the boat was hoisted and Kongre had the anchor raised.

From the top of the cliffs John Davis and Vasquez heard the regular noise of the pawl while the capstan hauled in the chain. After five minutes the anchor, being at the peak, was brought up to the cathead. Immediately the schooner began her maneuver. She had all her sails standing, high and low, in order not to lose any of the wind; then she finally got out of the inlet and, to catch the wind better, kept midway between the two shores.

In these circumstances, however, the navigation became very difficult. As the tide was still coming in, the schooner, sailing off the wind, was hardly gaining anything against the current, which would continue for two more hours, and would clearly not be off Cape San Juan before midnight.

But it did not matter. Since the *Santa Fe* was not coming into the bay Kongre did not risk an encounter. Even if he had to wait for the descending tide he would be out before sunrise.

Nevertheless, the crew used every trick in the book to increase the *Carcante*'s speed. Impossible to make her carry more sail since they had already set even the stay sails. But a very real danger appeared in her irresistible drifting, since the wind was slowly pushing her onto the right bank of Elgor Bay. Kongre was not well acquainted with it, although he knew it was dangerous, with a long trail of rocks where they risked shipwreck. An hour after leaving he considered himself so close that he decided to tack about and move further away.

Such a tacking against the current could not easily be done, especially since the wind was falling as night came on.

All the same it was becoming urgent to maneuver or else the *Carcante* would come too much under the wind. Accordingly the crew set to. With the helm alee, they hauled the aft sails taut while slackening the forward ones. But since her speed was insufficient, the schooner, hampered by the current, was not able to luff and continued drifting towards the right bank.

Kongre felt the danger. Only one option remained, so he took it. The boat was lowered, six men took their places, and managed to use the oars and a towline to turn the schooner into the starboard tack. For quarter of an hour she sailed for the left of the bay and could once more follow her original direction without fear of being thrown on the southern reefs.

But not a breath of wind could now be felt; the sails flapped against the masts. The boat would not have been able to tow the *Carcante* to the mouth of the bay against the rising tide. It could only have ridden it out until the tide turned.* Kongre would perhaps indeed be forced to anchor here for two hours even though he was only a mile and a half from the inlet.

When the boat had set sail, John Davis and Vasquez had stood up and, working their way along the top of the cliff, followed the schooner's movements. The wind had completely fallen and they understood that Kongre would be forced to stop and wait for the descending tide. But he would still have time to reach the mouth of the bay before dawn and so have every chance of slipping through unnoticed.

"We've got him!" suddenly exclaimed John Davis.

"How?"

"Come on . . . come on!"

And John Davis frantically dragged his friend towards the lighthouse.

To his mind the *Santa Fe* would have decided to cruise near the island and even come very close in—which presented no danger in a calm sea. It was clear that Captain Lafayate, very surprised the lighthouse was not operating, would be on low steam waiting for sunrise.

This is what Kongre thought as well; but he also said to himself that he had a good chance of giving the sloop the slip. As soon as the tide sent the water from the bay towards the sea, the *Carcante* could sail off again, even without a wind, and be off Cape San Juan in less than an hour.

Once out of the bay Kongre would not head for the open sea. He would only need a southerly current and one of those light breezes which occur even on quiet nights to follow the length of the coast in this pitch black night. As soon as the schooner had rounded Several Point, at most seven or eight miles away, she would be hidden by the cliffs stretching as far as Vancouver Point, and would have nothing more to fear. The only danger was of being spotted by the lookouts on the *Santa Fe*, if she stayed below the bay rather than at the mouth of Le Maire Strait. Surely, if the *Carcante* was sighted coming out the bay, Captain Lafayate would not let her get away, if only to question the captain about the lighthouse? Using her steam she would catch up before the *Carcante* could get behind the high southerly shores.

It was now after nine, and Kongre and his companions, having had to drop anchor to ride out the tide, now waited with great impatience for it to turn. The schooner swung in the water, her stem pointing for the open sea. However, her chain began to slacken and it would soon be time to weigh anchor. The boat had been hauled on board and Kongre would not waste a minute in setting off again.

Suddenly the crew uttered a cry, audible from both shores.

A long ray of light had just shot through the darkness. A beam was shining from the lighthouse with all its might, illuminating both the bay and the sea off the island.

"Agh! Those bastards are there!" exclaimed Carcante.

"All ashore!" ordered Kongre.

And indeed they had only this course of action to escape the great danger they were in: to land, leaving one or two men on board the schooner, rush to the enclosure, head through the annex, climb the stairs to the duty room, throw themselves on the keeper and his companions, if any, get rid of them, and extinguish the lighthouse. If the sloop had just started entering the bay she would surely stop

. . . if already in the bay, she would try to get out, without light to guide her to the inlet.*

Kongre had the boat moved alongside. Carcante and twelve of the men got in with him, bearing shotguns, revolvers, and knives. A minute later they were on shore, sprinting towards the enclosure—only a mile and a half away.

It took fifteen minutes to cover the distance. They had kept together. The whole gang, minus the two men left on board, reassembled below the plateau.

Yes, John Davis and Vasquez were there.

To reach the enclosure the two men had crossed the plateau as far as the barrier of rocks behind the beech copse—the very spot where the guanaco spotted by Moriz two months before had come to be shot. Then, sprinting across the prairie,* knowing no one was there, they had reached the foot of the enclosure.

John Davis had wanted to light the lighthouse once more so that the sloop could enter the bay and not wait out on the open sea. What he feared—and his fears had truly devoured him—was that Kongre had destroyed the lenses and broken the lamps and that the apparatus would no longer work. In such a case, the schooner would very probably be able to flee before being noticed by the *Santa Fe.*

The two ran to the quarters, found the corridor, opened the staircase gate, closed it behind them, climbed the steps, and reached the duty room.

The lantern was in good condition and the lamps in place, still equipped with wicks and oil since being extinguished. Kongre had not destroyed the lantern's dioptric apparatus, he had only thought of preventing the lighthouse working while he stayed at the end of Elgor Bay! How could he have foreseen the circumstances in which he would be forced to leave? And now the lighthouse was shining with all its brilliance and the sloop could return to her former mooring unimpeded.

But suddenly loud shots rang out at the foot of the tower. The whole gang had rushed inside the perimeter to climb up to the gallery and put the light out. All were prepared to risk their lives to delay the arrival of the *Santa Fe*. They found nobody on the terrace or in the quarters. There could not be many men in the duty room. They could overcome them easily, they would kill them, and the lighthouse would no longer shine ten miles around Staten Island.

It will be recalled that the gate at the end of the corridor was made of metal. To force the bolts was impossible. Also impossible to break it with handspikes or axes, and Carcante, who tried, soon realized and came back to Kongre and the others in the enclosure.

What to do? Could they climb up the outside and so get to the lantern? If not, the gang's only option was to flee inland to avoid arrest by Captain Lafayate and his crew. There seemed no point in going back to the schooner, and in any case they had no time, as the sloop would surely be already in the bay, steaming for the inlet.

There remained one way of reaching the gallery. If they could put the lighthouse out in the next few minutes, the *Santa Fe* would have to stop and even turn round and go back; in that case, surely the schooner could get past her?

"The lightning conductor!" exclaimed Kongre.

A cable indeed ran up the tower, with metal fixations every three feet. By hoisting oneself up from one to the other, it was possible to reach the gallery—and perhaps surprise those in the duty room.

Kongre started to try this last way out, but Carcante and Vargas had beaten him to it. They hoisted themselves onto the annex roof, took hold of the cable, and began to climb one after the other, confident they could not be seen in the dark.

Finally they got to the top, clung to the supports of the gallery, and now had just to scale it.

At that moment shots rang out. Carcante and Vargas, shot in the head, let go and fell onto the roof of the annex.

John Davis and Vasquez stood there, defending their position.

Whistles were then heard from the inlet. The sloop's siren was sending out high-pitched signals. The gang needed to get away. In a few minutes the *Santa Fe* would be at her old mooring.

Kongre and his companions, understanding the game was up, quickly dropped down from the terrace and ran off into the interior.

A few seconds later Captain Lafayate dropped anchor as with a few oar strokes the keepers' launch drew alongside.

John Davis and Vasquez went on board the sloop.

15. The End of the Story

The sloop *Santa Fe* had left Buenos Aires on 19 February* with the Staten Island relief team. Her journey proceeded very quickly, due to the favorable wind and sea. The great week-long storm had been restricted to Magellanic waters and not extended beyond the Strait of Magellan. Captain Lafayate had therefore been unaffected and reached his destination four days ahead of schedule.

Two hours later the schooner would have been far away in Le Maire Strait and they would have had to give up hope of pursuing Kongre and his gang.

Captain Lafayate did not want to let this night go by without knowing what had happened in Elgor Bay over the last three months.

Vasquez came on board, but not his colleagues Felipe and Moriz. Nobody had seen his companion before, and nobody knew his name. Captain Lafayate had them come into the wardroom, where his first question was:

"The lighthouse was lit late, Vasquez."

"It has not been working for nine weeks, captain."

"Nine weeks! And your two colleagues?"

"Felipe and Moriz are dead! Three weeks after the *Santa Fe* left the lighthouse had only one keeper!"

And Vasquez recounted the events on Staten Island. A gang of pirates under the orders of a certain Kongre had been living for several years on Elgor Bay, drawing ships onto the reefs of Cape San Juan, pillaging the wrecks, and murdering the survivors. Nobody suspected their presence while the lighthouse was being built, for they had hidden at Cape Gomez, the western tip of the island. Once the *Santa Fe* had left again, the keepers remained alone to look after the lighthouse. But three weeks later, at the beginning of January, the Kongre gang entered Elgor Bay on a schooner they had acquired at Cape Gomez. She had not been in the inlet more than a few minutes before Moriz and Felipe had gone on board and been struck down and killed. Vasquez was able to escape only because he happened to be in the duty room. After this, he had hidden on the shore of Cape San Juan, living off food taken from the pirates' cave.

Then Vasquez related how he had been lucky enough to save the first officer, following the wreck of the *Century*, lost at the mouth of the bay seven weeks later—and how the two men lived while waiting for the *Santa Fe*'s return. Their greatest hope then was that the schooner, delayed by major repairs, would be unable to sail for the Pacific before the sloop came back at the beginning of March. But she could have left if the two cannonballs John Davis fired into her hull had not caused a few more days' delay.

That is what Vasquez told Captain Lafayate, providing the slightest details he requested—having of course first presented to him the first officer of the *Century*.

The captain shook hands with John Davis and Vasquez, as their brave actions had meant the *Santa Fe* could arrive before the schooner sailed.

A few words of explanation will indicate how the sloop had reached Staten Island that very day, an hour before sunset.

Captain Lafayate had taken his bearings in the morning and was sure of his position, on the same latitude as Cape San Diego, at the southeastern tip of Tierra del Fuego.* When that cape was sighted to the west in the middle of the day, all the sloop had to do was head for Cape San Juan, normally visible as soon as she left Le Maire Strait.

Indeed when dusk began to darken the waters, Captain Lafayate made out very clearly the tall peaks standing up as the backdrop to the island, if not the east coast itself. He was then about fifteen miles away.

Almost two hours later, the *Santa Fe* was speeding towards Cape San Juan. The sea was calm, hardly affected by the last breaths of the sea breeze.

No doubt Captain Lafayate would not have been imprudent enough to approach the land so close at night, still less enter Elgor Bay and head for the inlet, before the Lighthouse at the End of the World had been built on Staten Island. But the coast and the bay were now lit up and he did not consider it necessary to wait until the following day.

The sloop therefore continued westwards and was only five miles from Cape San Juan at sunset. It was then that the *Santa Fe* had been spotted by John Davis and Vasquez who were observing the sea off the strait. She had also been seen by one of Kongre's companions, almost certainly from the top of the lighthouse. The pirate leader had then made arrangements to sail off as soon as possible and so get away before the *Santa Fe* reached Elgor Bay.

Meanwhile the sloop stayed at low steam. The sun had just disappeared below the horizon and the lighthouse was still not operating. An hour went by without light appearing over the island. Captain Lafayate could not have made a mistake in his position. Elgor Bay lay a few miles away. Although he was within range of the lighthouse the beacon was not lit!

On board the sloop they deduced something had happened to the apparatus. Perhaps some storm had been so violent as to break the lantern, damage the lenses, or put the lamps out of service. Never, no never, would the idea have crossed anyone's mind that a gang of pirates had attacked the three keepers, that these assassins had bludgeoned to death two of them, and that the third had had to hide to escape the same fate!

"I was uncertain what to do," said Captain Lafayate. "Night was falling, so I couldn't risk coming into the bay. I planned to remain out at sea until first light. My officers, my crew, and I were worried sick as we suspected something had happened. Finally the lighthouse came on soon after nine. It must just have been an accident that it didn't shine earlier. I forced steam and steered for the bay, and an hour later the *Santa Fe* entered it. A mile and a half from the inlet I discovered an anchored schooner, apparently abandoned. I was going to send a few men on board when shots rang out from the gallery of the lighthouse. We guessed that the crew of the schooner were attacking our keepers, who were defending themselves. A quarter of an hour later the *Santa Fe* was tying up at the inlet."

"Just in time, captain."

"Which we could not have done if you had not risked your lives to light the lighthouse again. The schooner would have long been on the open sea. We would probably not have noticed her leaving the bay and that band of pirates would have got away from us!"

In a flash the whole story was known on board the sloop, with the warmest congratulations going to Vasquez and John Davis.

After a peaceful night Vasquez met the three new keepers brought by the *Santa Fe*. It goes without saying that the same evening a large detachment of sailors had been sent to the schooner to secure her, for Kongre might easily have tried to board again and he could have quickly reached the high seas on the ebb tide.

To guarantee the safety of the new keepers, Captain Lafayate surely now had just one aim: to rid the island of the bandits infesting it. Even after the death of Carcante and Vargas, there were still thirteen of them, including a leader reduced to despair.

Given the size of the island, the search might be long and even unsuccessful. How could the crew of the *Santa Fe* search so many caves in the coastal cliffs and hiding places in the interior? Surely

Kongre and his companions would not be so careless as to return to Cape Gomez, for the secret of that hiding place might be out and in any case the cavern would have formed part of the searches. But it might be weeks or months before every last man was caught. And yet Captain Lafayate would not leave Staten Island until the safety of the keepers was guaranteed by the complete extermination of the pirates and the functioning of the lighthouse remained safe from any aggression.

It was true—and this would no doubt bring a quicker result—that Kongre and his men were destitute. They had no food left in either the Cape Gomez cavern or the Elgor Bay one. As far as the latter was concerned, Captain Lafayate, guided by Vasquez and John Davis, was able to confirm at dawn the following day that it held no reserves of biscuits or salted rations or indeed preserved food of any sort. All the provisions had been transported on board the schooner, which was now brought back to the inlet. The cavern now only contained salvage of little value—bedding, clothes, kitchen items—soon brought back to the quarters.

Even had Kongre come back at night he would not have found anything to help his gang. He very probably had no weapons because a variety of revolvers, rifles, and ammunition were found on board the *Carcante*. His only resource would be fishing and he and his companions would soon be forced to surrender if they did not want to starve to death.

Nevertheless searches were immediately initiated. Several detachments of sailors under an officer or petty officer headed inland and along the coasts. Captain Lafayate even traveled to Cape Gomez, but found no trace of the pirates.

On the morning of 6 March several days had passed and they had not found a single pirate. But that day, seven wretched Pécherais arrived at the perimeter, exhausted and starving. Taken on board the *Santa Fe* they were fed and locked up.

The following day, First Officer Riegal discovered five bodies on the coast near Vancouver Point, among whom Vasquez was able to recognize two of the Chileans in the gang. Clues showed they had tried to live off fish and crustaceans; but there were no hearths, charcoal, or ashes and clearly they had no method of making fire.

Finally, that same evening, just before sunset, a man appeared at the section of cliff overlooking the inlet.

It was almost the same place where John Davis and Vasquez had observed the departure of the schooner after the sloop had been first sighted.

This man was Kongre.

Vasquez, strolling in the enclosure with the new keepers, immediately recognized him, exclaiming:

"He's over there, *there!*"

At this cry Captain Lafayate, who was pacing the shore with his first officer, rushed up.

John Davis and a few sailors had run with him, and all assembled on the terrace, where they could see the leader of the pirates.

What had he come to do at this spot? Why was he showing himself? Did he intend to surrender? He could have no illusions about the fate awaiting him. He would be taken to Buenos Aires and pay with his head for a lifetime of pillage and murder.

Kongre remained motionless on top of the cliff. His eyes plunged below him into the inlet. Near the sloop he could see the schooner which luck had sent to Cape Gomez at just the right moment! And without the arrival of the sloop, which had prevented him leaving, she would have been in the Pacific for several days now—and Kongre and his men would have escaped all pursuit, knowing they could never be caught.

As can be understood, Captain Lafayate longed to capture Kongre. He gave orders accordingly and First Officer Riegal, with half a dozen sailors, slipped out of the perimeter towards the beech copse, from where they could easily climb the rocky outcrops and reach the plateau. Vasquez and John Davis showed this little troop the quickest route.

They had not gone a hundred paces before an explosion rang out on the summit. A body fell into the chasm and dashed against the rocks below.

Kongre had drawn a gun from his belt and pressed it to his forehead. The miserable wretch had administered justice to himself. The tide was already carrying his body out to sea.

Such was the denouement of this drama on Staten Island.

It goes without saying that since 3 March the lighthouse had been in continuous operation. The new keepers had been briefed by Vasquez. In any case not a single man from Kongre's gang remained.

As for John Davis and Vasquez, both were going to embark on the sloop for Buenos Aires. From there John Davis would be going home to Mobile, where he would soon undoubtedly obtain the command that his energy, courage, and personal qualities merited.

As for Vasquez he would return to his home town to rest after so many trials borne with such resolution. But he would travel alone—his poor colleagues would not be going back with him!

It was in the afternoon of 9 March that the *Santa Fe* made her preparations for departure. Captain Lafayate was leaving the new keepers in perfect security. And, like the last time he sailed out of Elgor Bay, the sea for eight miles around Staten Island was brightly illuminated with the light projected by the Lighthouse at the End of the World.*

Notes

1 to the west. A note in the margin of the manuscript, following
   Verne's habit of checking the chronology by marking the dates,
   reads: "9 Dec. 1859," with "18 April" in faint pencil above.

1 *Santa Fe*. Literally "Holy Faith," often associated with Catholic
   proselytizing. As Vairo points out, the ship (which Verne writes
   "*Santa Fé*") is probably named for the city of Santa Fe in Argentina,
   since the real-life vessel involved in the building of the 1884 lighthouse was the *Paraná*, and Paraná and Santa Fe are only ten miles
   apart.

   Jules Verne's manuscript (the basis for the present edition, henceforth: MS): "~~Santa Cruz~~ Santa Fe." The *Santa Cruz* (Holy Cross)
   was one of Lasserre's cutters on his 1881 expedition, named after her home port in Argentina, confirming Vairo's view that one
   source for Verne was the 1884 lighthouse. In contrast with Verne's
   single vessel, seven ships sailed to Staten Island to build the real-
   life lighthouse, as well as a prison, telegraph office, and subprefec-
   ture (although the latter was transferred to Ushuaia in Tierra del
   Fuego the same year).

1 Elgor Bay. Verne probably invented the name "baie d'El Gor," or
   rather borrowed it from his *Clovis Dardentor* (1896), where El
   Gor is a village in Algeria. Miller's map erroneously places Elgor
   Bay on the south coast. Vairo locates it in Port San Juan (de Salva-
   mento), between Cape San Juan and what was later called Punta

Lasserre, on the north coast of the island, the site of the 1884 one, strangely at the end of the bay. Verne does say that Elgor Bay is "about three miles long," which corresponds only to Port San Juan, and similarly places it three miles inland, but he also states that it is "on the east coast" (ch. 1), necessarily between Diegos and Several Points. Despite his dubious identification, Vairo (xiv) comments favorably on the accuracy of Verne's information about the only port after the Strait of Magellan, one frequently used by the French navigators and marked on charts as a place for repairs, with abundant water, wood, fresh meat, and wild celery to fight scurvy. Pétel's map correctly places Elgor Bay near modern Ferreyra Bay, just south of the northeastern tip.

1   Staten Island. Jack London has a striking passage about an approach to Staten in *Mutiny of the Elsinore* (1914, xxxii): "All of the land that was to be seen was snow. Long, low chains of peaks, snow-covered, arose out of the ocean. As we drew closer, there were no signs of life. It was a sheer, savage, bleak, forsaken land, a wild bight, between two black and precipitous walls of rock where even the snow could find no lodgment. I saw the four masts of a great ship sticking out of the water."

2   Captain Lafayate. The fleet to build the 1884 lighthouse was under a Colonel Augusto Lasserre.

2   Patagonia. Magellan invented this name "because the inhabitants, called Patagonians, that is 'men with big feet,' had long shoes made from guanaco skin" (*Magellania*, iii). On 3 December 1887, while discussing the possibility of a map for *Two Years' Holiday*, Verne wrote to his publisher, "Patagonia, as I told you, exists only on French maps. On the present map [in Spanish] and on the Yankee maps, Chile and the Argentine Confederation consider themselves to be at home as far as Cape Horn." If the term may formerly have had validity in all languages—it is used, for example, by Poe in *Arthur Gordon Pym* (xvi)—after about 1900 it was much less used because Patagonia had been split between Chile and Argentina.

In Verne's *Captain Grant's Children: Journey Around the World*

(1867), the brilliant but absent-minded French geographer Paganel cites "one of his compatriots who formerly occupied the throne of Araucania . . . the good M. De Tonneins [*sic*]" (I xi). Former lawyer Orelie de Touneins was famously elected King of Araucania and Patagonia in 1860, but was ousted by Chile in 1862, and subsequently mounted three expeditions to rally the Indians against the foreign invaders.

3   the Cape Horn seas are ill-famed. "That famous Cape Horn which, better than its brother the Cape of Good Hope, would have deserved the name of Cape of Tempests!" (*Grant*, I ix).

3   the number of wrecks on these coasts! Nearly one wreck a month was estimated to happen, or eight to nine hundred over the nineteenth century.

3   Cape Tucuman or Several Point. Verne refers to "cap Tucuman" and "pointe Several," both unattested. The latter is now known as Fallows Point.

4   the Magallanes. Verne's "Magéllanie" is normally "(the) Magallanes" in English, the term used here; "Magellania" was unattested until *Magellania* (2002), the English translation of *En Magéllanie*.

4   the morning. MS reads "11 October" in the margin.

4   Le Maire Strait. Named by James Le Maire (c. 1565–1616), Dutch navigator.

5   That year. 1859, as revealed in ch. 2.

6   Tierra del Fuego to Tierra de la Desolacion, between Cape Virgins and Cape Pilar. As Verne says in ch. 2, Cape Virgins (near modern Dungeness Point, Argentina) and Cape Pilar (Chile) represent the Atlantic and Pacific entrances to the Strait of Magellan. The area described is basically the islands off the tip of South America.

Volume 1 of *Grant*, which follows a line of latitude across South America, pioneers many of the elements of *Lighthouse*: Fuegians, guanacos, and "an unknown cataclysm which pulverized this huge promontory [Tierra del Fuego] cast between two oceans" (I ix).

7 "The double glazing keeps the wind out." In parallel with the next 150 words, the margin of the manuscript carries a different version in pencil, crossed out but legible.

9 the Strait of Magellan. Verne's *Two Years' Holiday* (1888) is set on real-life Hanover Island, less than ten miles from the Strait of Magellan, which provides "a shorter route than Le Maire Strait between Staten Island and Tierra del Fuego, and one less beaten by storms than that via Cape Horn" (*Two Years' Holiday*, xxvii).

9 Cape San Juan. Michel Verne [henceforth: MV] has a Gallicized "Saint-Jean" in place of the "San Juan" used by Jules Verne [henceforth: JV]. The cape, named by Noël Jouin from St. Malo (1706), was a synonym for shipwreck.

9 grazing the horizon. This ch. 1, with its display of self-conscious naval rituals, awareness of carrying the values of civilized existence, showing the flag, and triumphing over natural desolation, ironically underlines the evil soon to emerge from the shadows.

Michel concludes the chapter with a more poetic: "Captain Lafayate . . . gave the signal for departure. The sun was setting as he left the bay. / Suddenly a light shot out from the far shore, its reflection dancing on the wake. And the sloop, moving away on the darkened sea, seemed to carry with it a few of the incalculable rays projected anew by the Lighthouse at the End of the World."

2. STATEN ISLAND (PP. 10–18)

10 Staten Land. The name "Staten Land" was obsolescent even in 1859; the interest of the name is that Tasman's Staten Land (New Zealand) was conjectured to be part of a great southern continent stretching as far as Le Maire's Staten Land.

10 less than seven degrees from the Southern Polar Circle. A slip for "nearly twelve degrees."

10 Le Maire Strait . . . that name. *Grant*: "The Dutch Company of the East Indies . . . had an absolute right over all trade through the Strait of Magellan. / A few businessmen wanted to fight this

monopoly by discovering another strait . . . [and organized] an
expedition commanded by Jacob Le Maire and Schouten, a fine
sailor hailing from Horn. These bold navigators left in June 1615,
almost a century after Magellan; they discovered Le Maire Strait
between Tierra del Fuego and Staten Island."

10   about thirty-nine miles. About seventy-one kilometres. [JV]

       Staten Island . . . thirty-nine miles. This description is mis-
leading, for Staten Island runs east–west and Le Maire Strait more
or less north–south.

10   Cape Gomez . . . Parry Point to Vancouver Point. None of the
three localities has been traced. Parry and Vancouver Points may
be due to a misreading of the attested "Pto Parry" and "Pto Vancouver," since Spanish P^{to} (port) and P^{ta} (point) look similar. They
were named respectively for Sir Edward Parry (1790–1855), RN,
hydrographer and explorer who reached a record 82° 45' N in 1827,
and George Vancouver (1757–98), RN, explorer. Throughout the
book, MV replaces Verne's "le cap Gomez" and "la pointe Parry"
with what he identifies as the corresponding modern places,
"Cape St. Bartholomew," the southwestern tip of the island, and
"Cape Colnett."

10   Diegos Point. Verne's locality ("pointe Diegos"—cf. "cap Diegos"
on Tierra de Fuego [ch. 15]) has not been traced, although the
whole area was notorious for shipwreck.

11   The shore . . . is completely broken up. Verne often waxes lyrical
about complex coastlines, where land and sea come intimately together and untold mysteries lurk.

11   guanacos. Oxford English Dictionary (henceforth: OED): "a kind of
wild llama producing a reddish-brown wool, related to the alpaca."
Grant: "a fine creature, resembling a small camel without a hump;
it had a slender head, squat body, long slender legs, and fine light-
brown hair, with white patches on the underside of its belly. Paganel had scarcely looked at it before exclaiming: 'But it is a guanaco!' / 'What's a guanaco?' enquired Glenarvan. / 'An animal
that is edible.' / 'And is it good?' / 'Most savory. A dish of Olym-
pus! I knew that we would have fresh meat for supper!'" (I xiii)

Verne mentions the animal again in *Robur-the-Conqueror* and in *Two Years' Holiday* adds that it is far from "inferior to the most beautiful horses of American origin. You could certainly employ it for fast races if you first managed to tame it, then break it in, apparently child's play in the haciendas of the Argentine pampas" (xv). *Magellania*, especially, opens with a chapter entitled "The Guanaco" and a virtuoso five-hundred-word presentation similar to those of *Grant* and *Two Years' Holiday*: "long neck . . . squat body . . . elegant . . . with white patches." One source for the descriptions may be Bougainville, *Voyage around the World* (1772). However, the guanaco was already extinct on Staten Island by 1902 (Gerlache, 98), meaning the present tense in Verne's following sentence is misleading.

11   a few clumps of trees . . . Winter's bark . . . cinnamon. The descriptions of Staten Island flora and terrain are similar to some in *Magellania*, but emphasize its still greater ruggedness (Pétel, 209). Verne uses the unconventional and unattested plural "des écorces de Winter"; the bitter, medicinal bark was named for Captain William Winter, who sailed with Drake and used it to cure scurvy among his crew on the Strait of Magellan in 1578. MV writes "vanilla," a mistranscription.

12   feather-grasses. JV writes "stipals," no doubt a confusion between "stipas" and "stipel(le)s."

12   the Pécherais. Bougainville: "We . . . named them *Pécherais*, because it was the first word they pronounced on approaching us." OED cites only "W. Hodges, *Travels in India* (1793, 66)": "The wigwams of the torpid, wretched Pecherais [*sic*] on the frozen coast of Tierra del Fuego." In *Robur the Conqueror* (1886), the hero flies over the tip of South America, although the only description is: "It was the land of the Pécherais, or Fuegians, those natives who inhabit Tierra del Fuego" (xx).

13   the Fuegians. JV: "Fuégiens." OED lists seven occurrences of "Fuegian," starting with Weddell, *Voyage towards the South Pole* (1825, vi), and Darwin, *The Voyage of the Beagle* (1839, x). MV writes of

"Indians, catalogued under the name Fuegians or *Pécherais*, genuine savages on the last rung of humanity, living almost entirely naked and miserable, wandering over these vast solitudes" (*Jonathan*, I ii). Verne sometimes treats "Fuegians" and "Pécherais" as synonyms.

13 smelts. Smelts are normally found only in the northern hemisphere.

13 the Magellanic archipelago . . . the American continent. Since the division of the Magallanes in 1881 Staten Island has belonged to the Argentine Republic. [JV]

Magellania is similarly built on the fact that the Magallanes "belonged to no one and colonies could be founded there and retain their total independence" (iii). In the 1881 treaty, which remained controversial until the turn of the century, "this region lost its independence . . . Patagonia was annexed to the Argentine Republic, with the exception of a territory limited by the fifty-second degree of latitude and the seventieth meridian west of Greenwich . . . Chile renounced Staten Island and the less than half of Tierra del Fuego situated east of the sixty-eighth meridian. All the other islands . . . belonged to Chile" (*The Survivors of the Jonathan*, I iii; the text is absent from *Magellania*, JV's original manuscript, fundamentally changed by Michel). In sum, in 1859–60 when *Lighthouse* is set Staten Island is unclaimed territory—virtually the last on the globe outside the poles—although Verne never questions the Argentine presence there, or its ulterior motive of staking out its territorial claim.

14 the position chosen was the end of Elgor Bay. Verne omits to justify the inexplicable position of his lighthouse, presumably because there is none, apart from that of the 1884 model.

14 on this 9 December 1859. This is one of only two indications of year in the text. At the end of 1859, Verne himself was an impoverished art critic and playwright, newly married to a widow with two daughters. Throughout his career, many of his works, despite their absurd reputation for "anticipation," will hark nostalgically back to the 1850s, when Verne reached adulthood, escaped

Nantes, lived in the Latin Quarter of Paris, and researched intensively in the National Library.

14   four or five hundred square meters. Verne's system of measurements has generally been retained here. Nevertheless, since he uses both "meters" and "fathoms" ("toises"), the latter have been converted to the metric system for land distances, while retaining fathoms, cables, and (marine) miles for distances on the sea.

14   the annex. In ch. 1 Verne wrote "annexes."

15   eight miles. About fourteen kilometres. [JV] One paragraph below Verne reverts to "ten miles" as the effective range, surely a more accurate figure.

16   north-northwest . . . south-southwest in the latter. MV: "south-southwest . . . north-northwest"; the son also reverses many of the following compass directions. Dumas claims that Michel's change is "without apparent reason." In his other works, however, Verne confuses east and west scores of times, a surprising physical confusion for a writer with such a fundamentally spatial conception of existence (and for his editors, past and present, who often seem lackadaisical to the point of incompetence).

16   lenses. Verne leaves a gap here, filled by Dumas as "wicks" ("mèches"). However, since the same paragraph refers to "layered lenses . . . which contained a series of thin rings . . . all hav[ing] the same focus," "lenses" is used in the present edition.

16   a system similar to the Carcels'. The proper name is absent from the encyclopedias, with even the OED stating no information is available. In fact the person referred to is Bertrand Guillaume Carcel (1750-1812), a clockmaker who died in poverty, but gave his name to "a Carcel," a French unit of illumination, in competition with candle power. As shown by Carcel's dates Verne's technology was probably outmoded even in 1859.

17   the rod covers of the glasses. Dumas, following Michel, inserts "manchons," translated here as "rod covers," even if the term seems a little strange.

18   how could the gallery . . . the lightning conductor? Verne misleads the reader, hiding the final outcome behind a rhetorical question.

19 steamships and sailing ships more willingly venture. In French, "les NAVIRES vapeur et les voiliers s'aVENTUREnt plus volonTIERS," three anagrammes of "Verne" and an alliteration of *v*'s.

21 ten degrees centigrade above zero. Curiously enough, the cold, which in real life soon finished everyone off, has little impact in *Lighthouse*.

22 fed up or tired in twenty-four hours. Four paragraphs above the sloop had left Staten "days" before, and a page below, "five days ago."

24 a determined Nimrod. "the first potentate on earth . . . a mighty hunter" (Genesis 10: 8-9).

26 the *Montank*. The *Montank* was a Northern Monitor (ironclad) active in Chesapeake Bay in the Civil War, slightly connected with a famous murder attempt on President Lincoln, four of the plotters, including a woman, being executed.

29 "So there are hunters on the island?" An echo of *Uncle Robinson*, and its revised version, *The Mysterious Island*, in both of which the discovery of shot in an animal reveals a human presence on the island; in the latter case at least, this turns out to be Captain Nemo from *Twenty Thousand Leagues*. However, many of the "explanations" of the mysteries in the latter novel are either absent, as in this particular case, or manifestly absurd. Since many were due to the intervention of the publisher, this implies that Verne had doubts about the usefulness of what he was writing.

4. KONGRE'S GANG (PP. 30–40)

30 to the eastern end. MV replaces "eastern" with "western," an improvement.

30 calm weather. JV's sentence lacks commas, rectified by MV.

30 a detour of two or three miles. MV: "at least fifteen," again better.

31 The Chilean government, if it decides. MV corrects Verne's slip,

writing "decided." This sentence, alluding to the real-life Le Maire Lighthouse later built at the western end of Staten Island, is surprising, since Verne is naively suggesting it be built by Chile!

31   deep caverns. MV perhaps logically corrects this to "cavern." Given the large number of caverns, caves, grottoes, and hollows in the novel, it is worth identifying them. In this ch. 4, Kongre's gang live in a "spacious cavern," "twenty paces" from the angle of the cliff, just north of the mouth of Elgor Bay, at the eastern end of the island; a nearby cave serves for loot. While the lighthouse is being built, they retreat to the cave "near Cape Gomez," at the western end. In ch. 7 Vasquez spends one night in a "narrow crevice" "on the shore below the cliff"; later joined by Davis, he then lives in "a cranny, a small burrow of ten by five or six feet, near the corner of the cliffs on the shore of Cape San Juan," then in another, "five hundred paces" from it. In ch. 13 Davis and Vasquez move yet again, to a "hollow at the foot of the cliff," with the entrance a crack between rocks.

31   these dozen men . . . deputy. The number of bandits has grown to "fifteen or so" in ch. 4, then to sixteen in ch. 14, with eight men dying at the end and seven surrendering—which would imply one escaped, although the narrator affirms the opposite. "Kongre" may derive from an untranslatable French joke ("con-gre"), but more probably from "congre" (conger, a sort of large eel). The initial guttural *K* is often pejorative in Verne. "Carcante" perhaps comes from "carcan" (carcan, metal collar, especially for hangings).

32   Captain Dumont d'Urville . . . that name. The event happened in 1837, as recorded in *An Account . . . of Two Voyages to the South Seas* (Gallica, 1840). Jules Dumont d'Urville (1790–1842), explorer and naval officer, discovered the Venus de Milo and explored the Pacific and Antarctic, as extensively described in *Twenty Thousand Leagues* (I xix–xxii), but died in a French railway accident.

32   Punta Arenas. This town on the Strait of Magellan in southern Chile was a turbulent ex-penal colony, the base for the region's wreckers.

34 wreckers on the dangerous shores of the Old and New Worlds. Even a novel like Verne's *Underground City*, set in a disused Scottish coal mine, discusses navigation and in particular the "barbaric customs" of French wreckers: "Many wreckers on the Brittany coasts made a career from attracting ships to shore so as to share the spoils. Sometimes a clump of coniferous trees, burning through the night, guided a vessel into passes it could no longer leave. Sometimes a torch, attached to a bull's horns and moving with it at random, misled a crew as to the route to follow" (xiii). The theme undoubtedly derives from Verne's upbringing in a major port.

34 "a cargo worth several thousand piasters!" MV: "more than a hundred thousand piasters."

35 sufficed. The whole of the rest of this paragraph, from "which would have sufficed" to "New Hebrides," was added in the margin of the manuscript.

35 Then . . . the New Hebrides! The Gallimard Folio edition is defective here, omitting this sentence.

35 fifteen months. A slip for "fourteen."

36 removing the provisions. MV inserts "most of," more coherent.

36 Parry or Vancouver Points. In fact the work on the ship would not have been visible from here.

38 They would . . . 22 December. This sentence is far from clear, especially as the sloop had left on 10 December—presumably it refers to the supplies at the lighthouse. MV writes "enough for three or four days' march" and in the following pages makes several other chronological changes. After "22 December" he also inserts "already at the lighthouse. It was now . . . ," a clear improvement.

38 By leaving . . . inland route. The last seven lines, largely redundant, are cut by MV.

38 The day came . . . duty room. In the French text, the last three paragraphs are in the conditional tense (here partially attenuated), in a style specific to Verne—elsewhere he writes passages in the past conditional, to indicate what might have been (but

wasn't). The conditional here describes events yet to happen, in a sort of free indirect style reporting the thoughts of the characters. In the first two paragraphs, the thoughts are presumably Kongre's, but cannot be for the last three sentences of the final paragraph as he does not know the number or identity of the keepers. These sentences can only be ascribed to a more or less omniscient narrator, even if the events do not happen as described.

39   the 31st. MS reads "~~22nd~~ 31st," MV, "22nd." Dumas erroneously states that MV wrote "28th," and puzzlingly considers this the most plausible date.

40   whether she would succeed before night fell. Four lines above it is stated that "the vessel . . . would reach the strait before nightfall."

5. THE SCHOONER *MAULE* (PP. 41–49)

43   *Maule*, Valparaiso. The Maule is a major river valley in Chile.

44   Captain Pailha. Pailha is a rare French surname.

44   These islands . . . Tierra del Fuego. MV omits this sentence. In the Gallimard Folio edition there is a gap for the number of miles, filled in for the present edition.

45   the sea might not . . . half a cable towards the coast. This sentence is not clear since there is no reason for the ship to move "une demi-encablure" (one hundred meters) nearer the coast—perhaps Verne means half a fathom?

6. AT ELGOR BAY (PP. 50–60)

50   a complete success. "1 Jan. 1860" appears in the margin of the MS.

50   But . . . the open sea. Instead of these last three sentences Michel Verne writes: "She was too exposed to swells from the open sea and storms from the northwest."

51   a Chilean named Vargas. Stendhal has a "Duke de Vargas del Pardo" in the short story "Suora Scolastica," but Vargas is also a

town in Spain and means "misery" in Lithuanian, cognate of Norwegian "varg" (wolf, and hence criminal).

53   That would . . . to freshen. The French text seems strange here ("Cela dépendrait de la direction du vent, et non s'il se tenait dans le nord et tendait à fraîchir").

53   a green ray. A transparent allusion to Verne's Hebridean novel of the same name (1882), where seeing the green flash, a rare refractive phenomenon in which the edge of the setting sun momentarily turns emerald green, is a sign of true love. It is also echoed in the green ray that appears at the end of *Magellania*. The 1882 novel centrally proposes that those who see this ray are clearsighted as regards feelings and able to see into their own heart and those of others. But in *Lighthouse* there are no feelings, at least of the romantic sort, and in any case it is not clear whether Kongre and company even see the green ray.

54   She then headed east. Probably another slip for "west."

55   3 January. The year is 1860.

58   It was six o'clock . . . Elgor Bay. In the MÉR version, MV deletes "With the wind abreast," make a few other changes to this paragraph, and concatenates it with the following paragraph.

59   pirates. MV cuts the remaining words in this paragraph ("who . . . others").

59   lighthouse. MV replaces "entered it . . . lighthouse" with "entered it. Kongre headed in with the wind behind him."

59   to check. MV abbreviates "cave . . . to check" with "cave, Kongre and Carcante could check." However, he might have made "cave" plural, since the pirates should have checked that the storage cave was also still concealed.

59   forty-five minutes. MV: "twenty."

59   Accordingly . . . the lighthouse. MV omits this sentence, together with the following one and a half sentences.

60   A final cry. MV cuts this phrase.

60   Once . . . anchoring. MV adds "Perhaps they knew nothing of his existence, but" at the beginning of this sentence.

60   for the good reason . . . disembarked. MV cuts this slightly inelegant phrase.

7. THE CAVERN (PP. 61–69)

62   They all speak Spanish! Brazilians speak Portuguese!

64   The deep faith . . . their crimes. Verne often mocks any belief that God ever openly intervenes in human affairs, and resents organized religion, but seems to have been moderately Catholic. Positive religious references appear more frequently in *Lighthouse* than most of his other works.

8. REPAIRING THE *MAULE* (PP. 70–78)

70   waste no time. MS has "~~29 Dec. 3 Jan.~~" in the margin.

70   All in all . . . get the job done. Verne wrote this paragraph, plus the second sentence of the following paragraph, in the margin in a different writing. A crossed-out section includes "work in Valparaiso."

72   Had there been . . . more than three months. The ninety man-months of lighthouse provisions have grown since ch. 2, when the amount merely amounted to "six months of provisions" for three men.

72   between sunrise and sunset. A slip for "between sunset and sunrise."

73   four more days. One sentence before, the delay was "a couple of days."

76   follow the island's southern coast to Several Point. A slip for "eastern coast."

77   most fortunate. The vocabulary of this and the following paragraphs, including "fortunate" and "congratulations," encourages readers to identify with the pirates' endeavors.

9. VASQUEZ (PP. 79–88)

81   two or three weeks. Previously the estimate was "a good week or more."

89 Next day . . . as ever. MS: "~~18 Feb.,~~" the correct date.

91 Then Vasquez . . . ". . . avenged!" MV, an atheist, deletes these two paragraphs.

93 loosen . . . arms. This passage, with its "loosen the man's lips . . . changed the man's wet clothes . . . rubbed his chest and arms . . . supported him in his arms," contains homosexual innuendo.

93 John Davis. Probably an allusion to the Briton John Davis (c. 1550–1605), who made three voyages in search of the Northwest Passage (1585–87) and was killed by pirates in the Strait of Malacca. Verne cites him briefly in *Captain Hatteras* and extensively in *The First Explorers* (II iii). A Captain John Davis from Mobile features in *Traveling Scholarships*. Alexandre Dumas père, a friend and protector of Verne's in the 1850s, also wrote a sea novel called *The Adventures of John Davys* (1840).

96 Vasquez . . . earlier. As Riegert points out, the next five hundred words repeat, from the point of view of Vasquez rather than the narrator, the events already described in ch. 6. Furthermore, Vasquez narrates the same events again in ch. 15, to Captain Lafayate this time.

98 "plenty of wood from my poor ship!" The only way to stop wrecks is to make smoke signals—using wood taken from boats that have already been wrecked. Verne delights in closed cycles that either reinforce exponentially or self-devour down to the last crumb.

11. THE WRECKERS (PP. 99–109)

100 His soul . . . must have been bolted onto his body. The normal meaning of the French expression is "to have nine lives," but Verne reactivates the literal sense. The expression is too popular to occur in canonical French literature—the exception being Alexandre Dumas fils, Verne's friend, collaborator, and protector, who uses it regularly.

103 You win some, you lose some," replied Carcante. MV: "'Each new

shipwreck is different!,' replied Carcante philosophically. 'It's quite simple: we've been dealing with beggars.'"

104   It . . . left bank. Verne inserts this paragraph in the margin in a different hand.

105   As . . . the rocks. This paragraph repeats information from three paragraphs above.

108   it would not be long before a vessel could. JV's (and MV's) text reads "un bâtiment n'eût pas tardé à . . .," but makes little sense without adding "could."

12. LEAVING THE BAY (PP. 110–18)

111   the *Carcante*. For Jules Verne, unlike Michel, the *Carcante* is female.

113   They knew . . . three-master. Schooners originally had only two masts.

115   its rocks extended only a few fathoms into the deep water. This contradicts the previous paragraph.

116   the left bank. More logical would be "right bank"; Michel writes "north bank," which disguises the problem.

118   at about ten o'clock, the tide turned. Three paragraphs above Verne says the tide turns at "three o'clock."

13. TWO DAYS (PP. 119–28)

119   the others. MV changes the chapter title to "Three Days" and adds sections to develop the chapter, the first time since his father's death that he composes under his father's name, although his "Day of a Journalist in 2889" (1889) is also signed Jules Verne.

119   Elgor Bay . . .! In the French work, Verne uses nearly 500 ellipses (whereas Michel reduces the number to 384). Their main function is to indicate an incomplete or incoherent idea, but also to underline the import of what is being said. Their repeated use is designed to alter the rhythm of the prose and break up the convention of serially linked sentences with clear beginnings and endings. While a decision has been made here to radically reduce the

number of ellipses, a few have been retained in the present chapter, so as to give some idea of Verne's technique.

122   the end of the first week of March. Previously the sloop had been expected simply at the beginning of March, presumably since Vasquez's tour of duty ends on 8 March.

122   Those criminals . . . get away from them. Davis's logic does not seem consistent here, since previously the two had been prepared to lay down their lives to delay the schooner.

127   set out. As Dumas points out (Folio, 235), "MV inserts six pages at this point recounting Vasquez's attempts to blow up the rudder, which delays the schooner's departure another day."

14. THE SLOOP *SANTA FE* (PP. 129–38)

134   It could . . . turned. Verne's syntax is shaky here, for "it" (the boat) should logically be "she" (the ship).

136   if already . . . the inlet. Would it not be safer for the sloop to anchor than sail back in darkness?

136   the prairie. Although the prairie has been mentioned once as being near the enclosure (ch. 3), the layout of the plateau, the terrace, and the prairie is not clear.

15. THE END OF THE STORY (PP. 139–45)

139   The sloop . . . 19 February. MS has "8 March" in the margin.

140   Cape San Diego, at the southeastern tip of Tierra del Fuego. Verne wrote simply "Cap Diegos"; not the same as Diegos Point on Staten Island, but the site of a lighthouse on Tierra del Fuego Island, described as "San Diego, a sort of crouching sphinx whose tail bathes in Le Maire Strait" (*The Survivors of the Jonathan*, I ii).

145   brightly illuminated . . . the Lighthouse at the End of the World. *Magellania* has a very similar ending to *Lighthouse*: "and then escaped that ray of luminous green, the complementary color of the red that had disappeared. / At that moment the current sent from below caused an electric arc to leap between the plugs of the lantern, whose beams shone through the glass lenses and hence

to every point of the horizon. / The lighthouse had just cast its first flash on the Magellanic waters, and the *Yacana*'s two cannons greeted it with detonations amongst a thousand hoorays from the spectators. / And now when ships arrive from the east and sight the light of Staten Island at the extremity of the Fuegian coast, they can, before seeing the lights in the Chilean waters, get their bearings on this lighthouse of Cape Horn erected by the colonists of Hoste Island at the intersection of the Atlantic and Pacific."

In the Days of the Comet
By H. G. Wells
Introduced by Ben Bova

The Last War: A World Set Free
By H. G. Wells
Introduced by Greg Bear

The Sleeper Awakes
By H. G. Wells
Introduced by J. Gregory Keyes
Afterword by Gareth Davies-Morris

The War in the Air
By H. G. Wells
Introduced by Dave Duncan

The Disappearance
By Philip Wylie
Introduced by Robert Silverberg

Gladiator
By Philip Wylie
Introduced by Janny Wurts

When Worlds Collide
By Philip Wylie and Edwin Balmer
Introduced by John Varley

Also of Interest by Jules Verne:

The Chase of the Golden Meteor

The Chase of the Golden Meteor is vintage Verne, artfully blending hard science and scientific speculation with a farcical comedy of manners. This unabridged edition will be sure to delight Verne's legion of fans and attract new ones.

ISBN: 978-0-8032-9619-0 (paper)

The Meteor Hunt
The First English Translation of Verne's Original Manuscript

This is the story of a meteor of pure gold careening toward the earth and generating competitive greed among amateur astronomers and chaos among nations obsessed with the trajectory of the great golden object. Set primarily in the United States and offering a humorous critique of the American way of life, *The Meteor Hunt* is finally given due critical treatment in the translators' foreword, detailed annotations, and afterword, which clearly establish the historical, political, scientific, and literary context and importance of this long-obscured, genre-blending masterpiece in its true form.

ISBN: 978-0-8032-9634-3 (paper)

Order online at www.nebraskapress.unl.edu or call 1-800-755-1105. Mention the code "BOFOX" to receive a 20% discount.